UNBALANCED

A ZODIAC SHIFTERS PARANORMAL ROMANCE:
LIBRA

ANN GIMPEL

CONTENTS

UNBALANCED

A ZODIAC SHIFTERS PARANORMAL
ROMANCE: LIBRA

Wylde Magick, Book Three
By
Ann Gimpel

Dragon shifters clash in a blast of fiery heat.

Zachary Marston, dragon shifter, hasn't done a whole lot of shifting lately. Nope, he spends his time buried in law books as he presides over Superior Court in Denver. He's convinced himself things are great, but his dragon has other ideas. His bondmate is a tough adversary. After it threatens to abandon him, Zachary gives in and agrees to a meeting with a few other shifters. Maybe he can help out—before returning to his cushy courtroom.

Chloe's always longed for a bondmate of her own. After her twin brother links with a lion, she ups the ante, casting every spell she can think of, but none of them work. Even the smoking-hot dragon shifter who crosses her path can't ease the sting of remaining mateless.

Vampires are gaining strength, draining mage magic to augment their own. Shifters and mages—the good ones—have to mobilize fast. Libra to his bones, Zachary slings words Chloe's way, but she's a Leo and not intimidated by anything or anyone. They're an unlikely pairing, but destiny won't be denied. Like it or not, a shifter's mate is in the stars.

Seventh of the twelve Zodiac signs, Libra seeks peace, harmony, and cooperation. Symbolized by the Scales of Justice and ruled by Venus, planet of love and beauty, Libra is an interesting sign. On a good day, they can be charming, loveable, fair, sincere, and hopelessly romantic. On a less than good day, their manipulative, vain, indecisive, melodramatic, and narcissistic traits surface.

Like Gemini and Aquarius, Libra is an air sign. The essence of air is communication. Libras are smooth talkers who don't give up. They like to win and will wear you down with words. Libra is also one of the four Cardinal signs. As such, it kicks off the fall season. Cardinal signs prize originality and like to be first in what they do—no matter how high the cost.

CHAPTER 1

Zachary Marston glared at the lawyer standing in front of his bench. "You're wandering, counselor. Get to the point. Now."

The youngish man shifting from foot to foot colored. His dark hair was cut short, and his polyester suit practically screamed Men's Wearhouse. Despite his obvious discomfort, he didn't look away. Zachary—Zee to his few friends—offered the newly minted lawyer points for that.

"Sorry, Judge Marston. But I wanted to make sure the jury fully appreciates how valiantly my client struggled when her estranged spouse—"

Zee made a chopping motion. "Enough. Court is in recess until one o'clock." He eyed both attorneys, the one in front of him and a smooth, slick operator sitting next to his equally smarmy client a few feet away.

"Have your closing arguments ready when we reconvene. Ten minutes max."

Mr. Slick surged to his feet. "But, Judge. My arguments are prepared, and they're far more extensive than—"

"Cut them." Zee rose, judge's robes billowing around his tall frame, and turned. The bailiff held a door open, and Zee entered his chambers behind the courtroom.

"Do you need anything, sir?" the bailiff asked.

"Yeah. Solitude."

The corners of the bailiff's mouth twitched with suppressed amusement. "Easily arranged. No one will bother you through the noon hour."

Zee clapped the bailiff on the shoulder. "Thanks, George. Appreciated."

The bailiff turned liquid dark eyes on Zee. Gray stubble covered the top of his mostly bald head, and his face was a mass of wrinkles. As always, his beige uniform was crisp and pressed. "No worries, Judge. You and me, we go back a long way."

Before Zee could respond, George backed out the door, pulling it firmly shut behind him. Zee eyed the thickly padded black leather chair sitting behind a massive mahogany desk, but he was too keyed up to sit in it. He shrugged out of his robe and loosened his tie before crossing the room to large windows that looked out on the Rocky Mountains.

Denver's main courthouse was an enormous structure, complete with Doric columns and extensive lawns. The flower beds were empty this time of year, though, and the lawn had lost its summer lushness.

Deep within him, he sensed his dragon, his bondmate for the past 600 years. The creature was restless. He didn't blame it. He wanted to fly too, but his current life circumstances didn't offer much in the way of opportunity.

"Why are we doing this?" The dragon's question caught him by surprise.

"Doing what?" Zee kept his voice low. Not that his office lined with bookshelves and law books wasn't reasonably soundproof, but it paid to be prudent.

"This," the dragon repeated. *"Wasting time while you preside over small-minded wretches and their petty problems. Nothing you do changes anything. They walk back out into the world and do the same thing all over again. I liked it better on the other side of the big sea when you cut off hands or burned out tongues. Now those were deterrents."*

A smoke plume curled from Zee's mouth. He blew it aside and hoped fire wouldn't materialize next. Damn near everything in his office was flammable.

He had an uncomfortable hunch his dragon was

right—it almost always was. "What would you have me do?" he asked, keeping his tone mild. "The world has changed—a lot. Nowhere to go, really. Certainly nowhere we could fly free."

Thicker smoke billowed from his mouth and nose. "Stop that," he said. "If you set off the fire alarm, my office will turn into a zoo. I do not want the fire marshal and his minions racing in here with extinguishers."

"If it's the only way to pry you out of here, it's a grand idea."

More smoke. Zee batted it away and opened the window to offer an escape route.

"Okay. So we walk away from court in the middle of the day, leaving Mr. and Mrs. Shit-All-Over-One-Another without a judge to play Solomon. Where would we go?"

"You haven't been listening," the dragon huffed.

Zee didn't bother to tell his bondmate that he talked so much, sometimes Zee relegated it to background noise. "Which thing didn't I listen to?"

"The part about vampires on a rampage."

Zee sucked in a tight breath and gripped the polished wooden window sill. He had heard that part, but it felt enormous, daunting. Problems without evident solutions didn't appeal to him.

The dragon went on. *"The renegade mages who joined with vampires didn't help matters. But because of them, shifters and mages are finally working together again after pretending they barely knew one another since crossing the sea. Our place is with them. Fighting vampires. Not here."*

Heat pressed against his chest from the inside, and he opened his mouth to let steam bubble out. He'd kept to himself forever, mostly because his life was cleaner that way, less complicated. Hell, he'd been a judge in one capacity or another since the 1500s. And it had been a far simpler job back then, before the law became so complex it tripped over itself.

"I propose a compromise—" he began.

The smoke morphed into flames. He jumped back from all the wood surrounding the window and clapped a hand over his mouth.

"Goddammit," he swore and stuck singed fingers in his mouth to cool them. "Hear me out."

Without giving his bondmate another opportunity to intrude, Zee kept rolling. "We will finish today's case. Won't take long. We should be out of here by midafternoon. Then we'll go visit Angus O'Reilly at the feedstore. He always knows what's happening."

Zee frowned. A crusty Scot with a temper to match his red hair, Angus was as likely to chase him out of his store as to talk with him.

"And after that?" the dragon pressed.

Thank the goddess, no more fire billowed from his mouth on the heels of the dragon's question.

"After that, we take stock and see if this is even a problem where we could do any good."

"*It is!*" The dragon's words thundered through Zee's head, beyond the point of pain.

Zee shook his head briskly until his ears quit ringing.

"Let's listen to what Angus has to say before we get all spun out about this." Zee didn't add it was fifty-fifty Angus would toss him out on his ear. No love lost between dragon shifters and their kin who took other forms. He was fairly certain he was the only dragon shifter in North America. They were few in number, and the others preferred the northern reaches of the Asian continent.

Mostly, they were like him. Content with their hoards and solitude. Many were mateless, but they lived practically forever, so no one ever got too worried about them dying out.

He tugged on his tie and unfastened the top button of his shirt. His annoyance at the court proceedings faded to a distant spot, and he made his way around his desk to his chair. He thought about ordering lunch but wasn't hungry.

What kind of a can of worms was he opening if he visited Angus? Zachary was one of a handful of

Superior Court judges, a post he'd won via election. He was popular, well-loved. People forgave him his eccentricities since they were harmless. Like no wife or children.

He almost never entertained. What dragon wanted anyone anywhere near his hoard? And he didn't keep pets.

Shifters sometimes married humans, but not often. He'd fallen in love once, several hundred years before. Watching his beloved age and die had damn near killed him. It wasn't an experience he was anxious to repeat. People had longer lifespans now, but he didn't think it would be any easier to watch his partner die after eighty years than forty.

He'd moved to Denver twenty years before. It would be time to leave soon. Maybe five more years. Time to leave and craft a new identity for himself. It was a lonely life, but he had the law. Keeping up with new developments absorbed all the nooks and crannies of his spare time.

He liked the life he'd crafted for himself, but his bondmate didn't. Powerful, ancient, and canny, the creature hated being relegated to semi-oblivion. It retreated to the animals' special world from time to time, but that didn't take the place of spreading its wings and regarding Earth from an aerial perspective.

To smooth the way for later today, Zee picked up

his phone and hunted for the number of Angus's feedstore. A flash of relief surged when he found it. For all he knew, Angus had closed up shop and left.

Don't get too cocky, he cautioned himself. *Angus might have sold the business.*

He dialed the number. It rang four times, and then an automated answering machine picked up. Before it ran through the message, though, a series of clicks blasted Zee, and Angus's gravelly voice said, "Corner Feed."

Zee sucked in a breath. He'd been preparing to leave a message, but it wasn't an excuse to be out of words. "Hey, there, mate. How are you?"

"Fine, to be sure, but I'm not recognizing your voice."

"Zee, here. Long time since—"

"Cut the crap. What do you want? You must be wanting something, Zachary Marston, since I haven't laid eyes on you once these past ten years."

Zee tiptoed through a potential minefield, selecting his words carefully. He allowed the music of the Highlands back into his speech—something he'd worked hard to rid himself of—in hopes it would alleviate a few of Angus's reservations.

"I was hoping you'd have a wee bit of time for me later this afternoon. Mayhap around four?"

A long pause stretched. So lengthy, Zee checked the display to verify they were still connected.

"I might maybe could do that," Angus growled. "Question is why would I want to?" The wolf shifter had always been feisty and plainspoken, but this was a new level of rudeness even for him.

Zee relaxed his grip on the phone and shoved a desire to strangle Angus to a back burner. He adopted his best conciliatory tone, the same one he'd be using in his courtroom in a short time. "There's trouble afoot. Time to move beyond anything small that may have gone wrong between us and focus on the bigger picture."

"I don't need your fancy words."

"May I stop by?" Zee pressed. "I promise to leave all my ten-dollar words at the door."

"No dragon fire, either."

"I'm sure I can get my bondmate to agree to that." Zee squeezed his eyes shut and squashed the desire to keep talking until Angus capitulated. The wolf shifter had his number. Probably all his shifter kin did. He wore them down with one well-crafted argument after another until they gave in.

At least, he used to.

"Fine. See you around four." The phone clicked as Angus disconnected.

Zee stared at the screen before laying the phone on

his desk. "You heard that, right?" he queried his bondmate. "No fire."

"*Aye. I heard.*"

"And you'll comply, won't you?" Zee switched to Gaelic.

"*I'll do what's necessary. It may include compliance.*"

The dragon's presence retreated, and Zee raked his hands through his hair. He'd always figured his kin gave him a wide berth because of the dragon, but Angus's antipathy had been real.

They might not care for his dragon bondmate, but his fellow shifters didn't like him much, either. Why should they? He'd all but ignored them since his arrival in the Americas two hundred plus years before.

He winced. A decent-sized contingent of shifters lived in the Denver region. Not that they broke bread together, but some talked occasionally. At least, he assumed they did since no one ever reached out to him.

Unless they landed in some type of legal jam.

Not much you couldn't smooth over with magic, though. So, those types of emergency calls had been few and far between. Once the shifter was thinking rather than reacting, they understood they had everything they needed to extricate themselves from whatever mess they'd brewed up.

He ground his jaws together. He'd been helpful,

had never hung up on anyone either via phone or telepathy, yet he couldn't recall anyone ever thanking him. Or even closing the loop to let him know how things had come out. No one had ever ended up in his courtroom, or on the docket in another judge's, though, so he assumed his well-placed suggestions had borne fruit.

A brisk knock on his door signaled court would resume soon. Breath whooshed from him. Sometimes he enjoyed his job. Today wasn't one of them. Wealthy, battling couples in the throes of divorce disgusted him. Particularly ones like Mr. and Mrs. Shit-for-Brains whose only goal in life seemed to be screwing one another over.

He wondered what the hell they'd do to pass the time once the divorce was over and then decided he didn't give a damn.

His door creaked open, and George stuck his head around the corner. "Five minutes, Judge."

Zee stood and set his shirt and tie to rights. Snatching up the robe, he slipped into it. "Thanks. I'm ready now."

AT TEN MINUTES BEFORE FOUR, he parked his sleek, silver Mercedes a couple of blocks from the feedstore in a twenty-four-hour parking garage. He wasn't ashamed of his ride, but he knew in his bones that Angus would view it as pretentious.

The dragon had been quiet the remainder of the afternoon. No reason for it to nag further since Zee was doing what it wanted.

"*Now, remember,*" Zee reminded his bondmate as he exited and locked the car, "*no fire.*"

The dragon didn't answer.

Zee hurried down the sidewalk, aware he was overdressed, but there hadn't been time to go home to change. He'd removed his tie, but he was still garbed in a custom-made, dark-gray Italian wool suit with one of his many monogrammed silk shirts beneath the jacket. Shiny black pumps completed his "dress for success" look.

He pasted a smile he wasn't exactly feeling on his face and strode through the dirty swinging glass doors of Corner Feed. The shop looked deserted, so he headed toward the rear. His instincts were good. Angus stood, arms crossed over his chest, talking with Niall, a dark-haired jaguar shifter. Both men had longish, unkempt locks and wore denim jeans, long-sleeved Western shirts, and leather vests. A tall, well-built blond man Zee didn't know smiled pleasantly and held out a hand. Unlike the other two, the blond wore a dress shirt and trousers.

"You must be Zachary. My name is Jeremiah, and I'm pleased to meet you."

Zee shook the proffered hand, delighted at least someone had a grasp of manners. Once he let go, he offered a handshake to Angus and Niall. "Good to see you both." He nodded, still smiling and hoping his pleasant expression hadn't slipped too badly.

They touched hands briefly before Niall skewered him with intense dark eyes. "Angus said you're wanting to help? Is it true, or do you have some other agenda?"

"What other *agenda*"—Zee stressed the word —"would I be likely to have?" Acid etched his tone.

Niall shrugged. "Who knows, mate. I'm married now, as is Jeremiah. We have wives to consider."

"Congratulations." Zee's smile grew more genuine. "Who are the lucky women?"

"My mate is Sarai," Niall said.

"Ah, a wolf shifter and Stephan and Marie's niece," Zee replied. "Quite a beauty if I recall."

"Marie's dead," Angus said flatly.

Zee fell back a step. "How? We don't ever get sick, and she wasn't that old."

"Vampires." Jeremiah bit off the word, making it sound like the curse it was. "They kidnapped her and Stephan and Sarai. Marie fought back, and they drained her." His face developed a pinched look, and his blue eyes took on a grim cast.

"'Tis how we discovered vamps were drawing power from a willing batch of mages," Niall growled. "And the beginning of what's turned into a one-way trip into Hell." He squared broad shoulders. "If you're willing to throw in your lot with us, we could use your magic and your logic."

"We'd need all of you." Angus narrowed his eyes. "None of this judge-by-day, shifter-by-night crap."

Zee set his mouth in a thin line. "You're still working," he observed.

"Not really," Angus replied. "Aye, sure and I'm here, but 'tis turned into a convenient central meeting point. All I have to do is change the sign over the door from open to closed, and I'm free to leave."

"Are you really a dragon shifter?" Jeremiah asked, fascination laced into his question.

Zee mock bowed, low and sweeping. "Indeed. At your service." He looked Jeremiah up and down. "I thought I knew all our kin, yet I don't recognize you."

"That would be because I was a mage until quite recently."

Zee was used to concealing his reactions—to everything—but his eyes widened as he absorbed the unlikely statement. "How is that possible? Niall said you were mated? Is she one of us?"

"I told you he was more trouble than his magic is worth," Angus muttered and crossed his arms over his barrel chest.

Jeremiah held up a hand. "None of you were all that accepting of what happened to me, either. Not at first."

It registered the tall blond man was standing up for him. Zee had always fought his own battles, and it made him uncomfortable.

Before he could thank Jeremiah, but clarify he was capable of defending himself, a bell dinged from the front of the store, followed by a rush of footsteps. Zee scented the air. Women. Three of them. Two shifters and a mage.

Vampire rot clung to them, and his dragon snapped to attention. Smoke blasted from his mouth.

"I said no fire," Angus gritted out.

Zee rode herd on annoyance. If vampires were afoot, they needed to fight. Dragon fire killed vampires, and Angus was a fool not to recognize it. Sarai, Renee, and a woman he didn't recognize charged around a corner. Zee readied himself despite Angus's warning, but they were alone. They might stink of vamps, but none accompanied them.

The women wore scuffed leather boots, snug-fitting trousers, and warm, puffy jackets. Sarai's red hair was drawn into a queue. Renee's blonde locks hung in a welter of curls. The other woman, tall, broad-shouldered, and blonde, held herself like a queen.

She made a beeline for Jeremiah and planted herself in front of him, hands on her hips, elbows akimbo. Worry laced with determination shot from her blue eyes.

The dragon's attention did a rapid about-face, enthralled by the Valkyrie spitting exasperation. *"That one,"* it rumbled. *"We need that one."*

"She's a mage. Not for us." Zee shushed his bondmate, grateful no one was paying attention to him or his telepathic conversation.

Renee hooked a hand around the other blonde's arm. "Take it easy. He's my mate."

"What happened? Out with it. Why do the three of you reek of vampire?" Jeremiah screwed his face into a worried expression. "I've only been gone half an hour. What could possibly have gone wrong?"

Niall hurried to Sarai's side and wrapped an arm around her. "Sweetheart. You're shaking. What the bloody fucking hell happened?"

"Three mages came calling. No one we knew well, thank the goddess, but they weren't what they appeared. Once we invited them inside, they dropped their illusion and revealed themselves as vampires." Sarai leaned into her mate.

Jeremiah made a hissing sound. "Crap. Give me everything. Who's hurt? Who's—?"

"We're all okay. We killed them." The other blonde spat the words like bits of shrapnel. "Not us—or we'd be covered in that stinking crap that passes for their blood—but Raul, Johnny, and Liam beheaded them."

"We came as fast as we could to bring you back." Renee had moved to Jeremiah's side.

"Who the hell are you?" The Valkyrie had finally noticed Zee.

"Zachary Marston, dragon shifter, at your service." He inclined his head.

Sarai and Renee's heads swiveled as they, too, regarded him. "Been a while, dragon." Sarai sounded as friendly as a feral cat.

"Mmph." Renee rolled her eyes.

"Piss on your fancy words. Are ye in or out?" Angus aimed his question at Zee.

"Aye, decide now," Niall cut in. "We're heading to Silverthorne where the rest of us are. Got to get back in case more vamps show up."

"Except we're not stupid enough to invite anyone else inside," Renee snarled.

"If they're masquerading as mages, it means they located more of my erstwhile kin to mesmerize." Jeremiah clenched his fists and punched the air with one. "Bastards. Infernal bastards."

The blonde warrior's visage softened. "Brother." She placed a hand on Jeremiah's arm. "I'm sorry. After we killed so many of our own, I'd hoped—"

He cut the flow of her words with a stern glance. "No point living in the past, Chloe."

Zee send a thread of magic snaking outward. The two were indeed sister and brother, never mind one was mage and the other shifter. And the stunning blonde had a name: Chloe. He culled through his memory banks, hunting for information about mages, but Niall interrupted.

"Come with us now or leave, Zee. No time for the lengthy explanations you love so much."

He winced. "Shoot me an image or coordinates. I'll be right behind you."

"Nay. If you're coming, we'll include you in our travel spell." Power bubbled around Niall as he summoned magic. The air thickened and developed a multihued aspect.

Unused to ceding control to anyone, Zee hesitated. Silverthorne wasn't all that far. Maybe he'd be better off driving—

"*We're going with them.*" The dragon forced their magical center open, linking with Niall's spell.

"Excellent." Niall grinned, and for a moment he looked like the cocky, carefree jaguar shifter Zee remembered.

Zee let the magic swirling through the room snap him up. He had to admit he was curious about the vampire threat. Not much interesting had happened in the past couple of centuries. That was about to change, and the prospect intrigued him.

Beyond whatever was afoot, Chloe would be in Silverthorne too. She was a mage, but despite what he'd told his dragon, he wanted to find out more about her. A whole lot more.

He never took vacations; the law was his life, or it had been until today. Maybe now was the time to lie his head off about a family emergency. The more he thought about it, the better he liked the idea. He could easily clear the decks for three to four weeks. By then, he'd be ready to pick up the reins of his judgeship—or quit for good.

The dragon's approval sluiced through him, sticky and viscous, before it seconded, *"Quit for good."*

Zee snorted. His bondmate was in rare form, but perhaps it was long past time to listen to it.

n hour before:

Chloe Fuller was upstairs in her room in a rambling Victorian mansion when shouts rang out from the first floor. She yanked her door open and pelted through at a dead run but stopped short when she ran into a veritable wall of vampire reek. Rotten eggs mingled with decaying flesh and putrefying vegetation into a nauseating mélange. Why the hell did the bastards have to smell so bad.

"Because they're dead," she ground out through clenched teeth. "And dead shit stinks."

Sarai, a wolf shifter, and Renee, an eagle shifter, crested the stairs. Both women appeared rattled, but vampires had that effect. Sarai's red hair was braided, and her blue eyes held harsh edges. Renee's blonde hair floated around her to waist level. Her greenish eyes looked haunted, as if she'd peered into something far worse than Dante's Inferno.

"There you are." Sarai was panting, probably to cut the stench by breathing through her mouth.

Chloe swallowed back bile. "Vampires! How the hell did they get inside our house?" She clapped a hand over her nose. "Never mind. Let's go. We need to fight—"

"Not anymore. They're dead," Renee announced, sounding satisfied. "Niall's iron blades came in handy."

"I am so freaking glad we had the foresight to put them out in plain sight," Sarai cut in.

"Still doesn't explain how they got inside." Chloe chewed her lower lip. "Besides, it's not night yet. How are they doing anything..." Her words ran down since the answer was obvious.

"Figured it out, did you?" Renee shot a pointed look her way.

"No other explanation," Chloe muttered, although the words felt like chunks of stone as they fell from her lips. "They found more mages."

"Not that you're all that hard to locate." Sarai winced. "Sorry. That didn't come out quite right."

Chloe bristled and shoved hair out of her face. "I figured after we got the message out to all the mages who showed up for your mating ceremony, they'd spread the word, and—"

"And what?" Renee inquired caustically. "It's not as if we wiped out all the Mages First members, the ones who want to smear their bootheels with shifters."

Raul, the mages' healer, chugged up the stairs. "Why are you still here?" he demanded. "Between Liam, Johnny, and me, the vamps are dead. Go get Niall and Jeremiah. Bring them back. Angus too, if he'll come." Tawny hair streaked with gray fell to his shoulders, and his hazel eyes glinted with fierce determination. His jeans and gray corduroy shirt were splotched with vampire ichor.

"Sorry," Sarai said. "I know we were supposed to grab Chloe and be gone straight away."

Chloe's eyes widened as the implication sank in. She hadn't been aware her brother was gone. "Did you know Jeremiah left?" she asked Renee.

The green-eyed blonde nodded. "Angus got hold of him and Niall and asked if they'd show up for a meeting."

"What kind of meeting?" Chloe dropped the hand she'd been pinching her nostrils shut with. "I thought none of us were supposed to be alone—ever."

"Niall figured it would be okay since he and Jer were together." Sarai defended her mate.

"You still haven't told me what was so important," Chloe persisted.

Sarai blew out a tight breath. "Zachary, a dragon

shifter who's been peripheral to the fold forever, contacted Angus and was supposed to show up at the feedstore at four."

"So? Why would that be occasion for—?"

Sarai chopped a hand downward. "Dragon shifters are rare. Zachary's very old, and his magic is powerful. It might be a very good thing he recognizes it's time to own what he is."

"Or very bad," Renee said sourly. "That one, he marches to his own tune. Always has. I'd bet my last feather he has an ulterior motive that's all about him."

"Sounds like you're not fond of the dragon shifter," Chloe observed.

Sarai shrugged. "If you like the gorgeous, talkative type, he's okay." She turned her hands palms up. "He's a Libra. Kind of says it all."

"Not to me, it doesn't." Chloe's words were sharper than she meant them to be. Sarai ate, lived, and breathed astrology, while Chloe wasn't nearly as well versed in its finer points.

"Zachary—except we used to call him Zee—is a talker," Renee said. "He'll argue a point into the ground and follow it ten feet under. He's a judge, and it's probably a perfect job for him."

Chloe thought about it, but not very long. "I know you shifters have maintained a few degrees of separation from one another. I take it this one took it further."

Sarai nodded. "I never exactly got the impression he was ashamed of what he is, but he went to a lot of trouble to put distance between himself and the rest of us." Her gaze frittered skyward. "I bet it's been ten or fifteen years since I laid eyes on him. Outside of on television when he's presided over some splashy case."

"Never mind him. Get moving." Raul didn't raise his voice, but his tone was lined with urgency.

Until he spoke, Chloe had almost forgotten he was still standing there. "Thanks. We're all over it."

"I'll handle the spell." Power rose around Sarai before she was done speaking. "We'll be back before you know it. Meanwhile—"

A blast of harsh laughter blatted from Raul. "We don't have any plans to open the door. To anyone. Much less invite them inside. Goddess's tits, what the fuck were we thinking?"

"That they were mages, just like they appeared," Renee muttered just before the spell caught them up and the third-floor hallway ceded to blackness.

Chloe sucked in an anxious breath. She'd always been proud of being a mage, but what was turning into a mass defection by her kin shamed her. How could anyone steeped in mage magic join forces with vampires? Even having them in proximity made her feel like she'd taken a bath in slime.

She'd been part of a group of mages and shifters who had called mage fire to destroy over fifty shackled mages a few weeks before. The image of that day was burned into her brain, and it still haunted her dreams. Mages were a peaceful people. Killing went against the grain. Shifters were their magical cousins—a fact most of them had conveniently forgotten during a long-running war in the Old Country.

Cousins be damned; shifters were tougher than mages. They'd drawn the warrior gene, while mages were more dreamers and philosophers. The black of Sarai's travel spell shaded to gray, and Chloe forced her attention back to the present.

They were almost at the feedstore in downtown Denver. She'd have to tell Jeremiah about yet more mages being corrupted by vamps, and the news would damn near kill him. At least he had Renee, his brand-new mate, to soften the blow.

Still, he'd be devastated.

The cloudy glass doors of the feedstore shimmered into view. It took her a moment to realize they'd come out on the street side.

"Sorry," Sarai mumbled. "Slight miscalculation. I covered our entrance with magic. Hopefully no one noticed."

"Since I don't hear screams, you probably managed fine," Renee said tartly.

They pushed into the store and hustled toward Angus's small office in the rear. A wolf shifter, he was closed off enough Chloe didn't know him at all beyond the perpetual frown he wore. It was as if he was mad at the world and had been forever.

She made a beeline for Jeremiah and planted herself in front of him, hands on her hips, elbows akimbo. Once there, though, she was at a loss for words. No matter what she said, it would flay her twin brother's skin from his bones.

Renee hustled forward and hooked a hand around her arm. "Take it easy. He's my mate."

"And my brother. What? Do you think I don't love him too?" Chloe dragged her arm out of Renee's grip.

"What happened? Out with it. Why do the three of you reek of vampire?" Jeremiah screwed his face into a worried expression. "I've only been gone half an hour. What could possibly have gone wrong?"

Niall wrapped an arm around Sarai. "Sweetheart. You're shaking. What the bloody fucking hell happened?"

"Three mages came calling. No one we knew well, thank the goddess, but they weren't what they appeared. Once we invited them inside, they dropped their illusion and revealed themselves as vampires." Sarai leaned into her mate.

Air hissed through Jeremiah's teeth. "Crap. Give me everything. Who's hurt? Who's—?"

"We're all okay. We killed them," Chloe clarified. "Not us—or we'd be covered in that stinking crap that passes for their blood—but Raul, Johnny, and Liam beheaded them."

"We came as fast as we could to bring you back." Renee added and edged to Jeremiah's side.

Chloe had been so focused on Jeremiah, she hadn't noticed the tall, commanding stranger standing off to one side. Hair like living fire was drawn into a queue behind his head. Dark blue eyes nested beneath bristly brows. He was handsome in a rough, outdoorsy way despite his fancy clothes. Stubble was just beginning to shadow his squared-off chin.

Her earlier conversation with Sarai and Renee came roaring back. This must be the dragon shifter all the fuss was about, but he wasn't anything like Sarai's description. Or Renee's. Neither cold nor distant, he fairly oozed a sensual appeal that made her want to close the distance between them. To mask her totally inappropriate reaction, she growled, "Who the hell are you?"

"Zachary Marston, dragon shifter, at your service." He inclined his head and bowed.

"It's been a while, dragon." Sarai's opinion of him was obvious from her tone.

Renee huffed and rolled her eyes.

"Piss on your fancy words. Are ye in or out?" Angus aimed his query at Zachary.

"Aye, decide now," Niall cut in. "We're heading to Silverthorne where the rest of us are. Got to get back in case more vamps show up."

"Except we're not stupid enough to invite anyone else inside," Renee snarled.

"If they're masquerading as mages, it means they located more of my erstwhile kin to mesmerize." Jeremiah punched the air with a clenched fist. "Bastards. Infernal bastards."

Chloe's heart hurt for her brother, and she placed a hand on his arm. "I'm sorry. After we killed so many of our own, I'd hoped—"

"No point living in the past, Chloe."

Niall clapped his hands together once. "Come with us now or leave, Zee. No time for the lengthy explanations you love so much."

The dragon shifter made a face. "Shoot me an image or coordinates. I'll be right behind you."

"Nay. If you're coming, we'll include you in our travel spell." Niall shaped power, the air glowing as he worked magical strands to do his bidding.

"All right. I'm in," Zachary said, but he sounded more resigned than willing.

"Excellent." Niall added a smidge of fire to his spell.

"I'll join the lot of you later," Angus said. "I need to get the word out about this latest event."

"Sure you'll be all right?" Jeremiah clapped Angus on the back.

"Quite sure." He grinned, all teeth and zero warmth. "I'm too tough for those abominations to fuck with."

It was the first reaction other than anger Chloe had seen from the wolf shifter, and she hoped his assessment was accurate. He might be crusty and dour, but she didn't want harm to befall him.

Niall's casting swept them up, strong and sure. Before she had a chance to do much of anything, the walls of the downstairs great room formed around her. "Why'd your magic work so fast?" she demanded.

"Sure and I'd love to tell you a lie, enhance my own magical acumen as it were, but I had help." He crooked a finger in Zachary's direction. "Dragons are the strongest among us, and he opened his magic to me."

"Thank my bondmate for that," Zachary growled. "I was still leaning toward taking my car."

Much to Chloe's surprise, Niall inclined his head. It was a genuine gesture, not sarcastic or patronizing. "I offer thanks to your dragon for its wisdom and cool head."

Smoke puffed from Zachary's mouth, followed by steam. Chloe fell back a step. Hearing the man was a dragon shifter and seeing actual evidence were two different things entirely.

Puddles of ichor stained the places the vampires had fallen, but their bodies were gone. "What happened to them?" She directed her question at Raul.

"Two of them decayed almost immediately. We dragged the bones out back and incinerated them. Third one wasn't as old, so it was, erm, fleshier. Tossed it on the pyre along with the other two and used magic to disguise the smoke."

"Too bad getting rid of that goddess-be-damned reek isn't as easy," she muttered under her breath.

"Who wants to catch me up?" The dragon shifter's voice was a rich, mellow baritone, and he stood with the tips of his polished loafers a scant inch away from a pool of vampire goo.

Chloe almost leapt forward, wanting any opportunity to interact with the gorgeous redhead, but she reined herself in. Another shifter should be the one to step into the breach.

Except no one did.

"Why do you need catching up?" Sarai trained her blue eyes on him. "Isn't it obvious from context?"

Zachary crossed the space between them and stood almost toe to toe with her. "Nay, Sarai Lurie, it isn't. If it was, I'd not have wasted breath nor time on the question."

His speech, which had been pure American, now held overtones from the Scottish Highlands.

Niall stepped between his mate and the dragon shifter. "Sure and 'tis a reasonable request," he murmured. "Shall we retire to the dining room for a wee snack? Always easier to chat over food and drink. Plus, it won't smell as bad in there." He held out a hand.

Zachary clasped it. "Thank you for that, Niall MacLier. For a span of time there, I was certain manners had fallen out of fashion." Power shimmered around him, forming a glistening shroud. "I'll take care of obliterating the rest of the vampire residue, and then I'll gladly break bread with you."

The scents of heather, gorse, and lilacs rose around Zachary. As the smell of his magic grew, absorbing and obliterating what was left of the vampire spoor, Chloe took a step toward him. And then one more. If she didn't do something, she'd end up in the magical circle eddying about him.

"I'll get something ready for everyone," she called and sprinted for the kitchen. The longer she spent in the dragon shifter's presence, the harder it was not to grab any excuse to talk with him, get to know him better.

To hell with getting to know him. I want to strip his clothes off, and—

She put a lid on her overactive libido. He wasn't here for her. No. He was here to aid their cause, and she needed to keep that niggling little point front and center in her head. Or maybe he was here for some subversive, self-serving purpose only he was privy to.

Regardless, she'd do well to adopt a low profile until after he went home. Assuming he did. Awk. He had to return to wherever he called home. What the hell would she do if he moved in with them?

Don't borrow trouble. He seems quite independent.

She inhaled deep, blew it out, and did it again. Part of her wanted him gone ten minutes ago, but another, much bigger part wanted him to stay forever.

Chloe busied herself in the kitchen, grateful no one bustled in offering to help. She wouldn't have been very good company. The embarrassment that had rocked her earlier was back in spades. Her kin who'd signed on with vampires were a disgrace, but the problem wasn't going to go away. Not anytime soon.

Her confused welter of reactions to the dragon shifter wasn't going away, either.

As she chopped and arranged things on plates, ferrying them through swinging doors into the dining room, she longed for a bond animal of her own. Was it because she was disgusted with mages and no longer wanted to be one? Or was it a retreat to the desire she'd had as a girl for a bond animal to join its life to hers?

She didn't have an answer. After Jeremiah ended up bonded to a cave lion, she'd cast spell after spell in hopes of luring her own animal. Not necessarily a lion. She wouldn't be picky. She'd be thrilled with any bond animal at all, but none had heeded her magic—or her inducements.

Jeremiah hadn't had to do anything. The lion picked him and had broken through, making its presence known. Insofar as she knew, no other mage had turned into a shifter despite Sarai's prediction such alterations would become far more common.

In the weeks since her twin brother's transformation, she'd alternated between working magic and waiting impatiently. Neither strategy worked, and she was flat out of ideas, but nowhere near giving up. She wanted a bondmate and wouldn't rest until she had one—or received a clear message from the gods or the universe she was wasting her magical energy on a lost cause.

On her sixth trip into the dining room—or her tenth, she wasn't keeping score—Jeremiah said, "Chloe. Stop running back and forth to the kitchen like a demented rabbit. Sit down and take part in the discussion. If anyone wants anything else, they can get it themselves."

She sent an annoyed look skittering his way. "Demented rabbit?"

"Eh, poor choice of words. Sit down."

Just to make sure he didn't think he had the upper hand, she made one last trip into the kitchen, returning with the plate she'd been nibbling from and a glass of cabernet. With a pleasant nod, she slid into one of the vacant seats at the long, polished table that could seat twenty. She picked a location as far away from the dragon shifter as she could get, but his energy pricked her, made her uncomfortably aware of how skin stretched across her body.

What would his hands feel like stroking her peaked nipples? Or her stomach? Or lower still? She ripped the next lascivious image out at the roots. What the hell was wrong with her? He was a hunk, but it was no excuse for the lust leaking out her pores.

"Fascinating," Zachary was saying. "I do recall when we were one people with our mage kin, but my memories of the war are far fresher." He turned to face Jeremiah. "'Tis sorry I am to hear about the shackled mages. Burning them where they lay must have torn your heart out."

"It did." Jeremiah nodded sadly.

"What are your thoughts about how to proceed?"

Zachary let his gaze linger on each of them in turn as if they were important to him.

Chloe wanted to believe he cared when his eyes, with irises the color of a restless winter ocean, settled briefly on her, but she recognized a well-polished act. One he'd probably perfected during mediations or other courtroom exercises.

"Why are you really here?" Sarai asked Zachary. The clunk of a truth spell draped around the table. Sarai wasn't even trying for subterfuge.

Zachary adopted an injured look. "Was that truly necessary?"

"I thought so, or I wouldn't have bothered. I'm not in the habit of squandering my magic." Sarai sat straighter, rolling her shoulders back. "You're Libra through and through. I did a quick double-check on your chart earlier. That courtroom where you've sequestered yourself is perfect. It fills all your needs for endless discourse in the pursuit of truth. I want to know what you're doing here. And why your shifter kin have suddenly become a priority."

Everyone in the room zeroed in on the dragon shifter. He had the good grace to study his hands before making eye contact again. "My dragon was quite clear our magic is needed. Sometimes I can argue my bondmate out of things, but this wasn't one of those times."

He pushed to his feet and paced to the head of the room where he could see the nine mages and five shifters and spread his hands in front of him. A plain gold ring graced his index finger, curling around it much as a serpent would have done.

"My magic is strong, and it's at your disposal. I'm planning to request a sabbatical from my judgeship. Perhaps a month at first. If I need to be gone longer, I'll quit."

Steam billowed from his mouth, and Zee grinned. "My dragon likes that plan. It's been trying to pry me out of my courtroom for a long time."

Sarai tilted her head to one side. "You spoke true." A wave of her hand, and her spell dissipated.

"I would have even absent your casting." A corner of his mouth twisted downward. "If we're to work together, we must trust one another. I'm not sure what I did to make so many of you dislike me, but I stand ready to rectify it. I cherish my shifter heritage. If anything I've done or said through the long years of my life repudiates that, I am most humbly sorry."

"Good enough for me." Niall sprang to his feet and ran lightly to Zachary, hand extended.

The dragon shifter shook his hand and clapped him on the back. "Good. Now we're past that part, how do you propose to dissuade any more mages from joining forces with vampires?"

"Why not focus our efforts on the vampires and forget the mages?" Raul asked.

"'Tis a good question," Zee said. "Here is my rationale. Vampires have always existed. They began when Sekhmet, Egyptian goddess of death and destruction, made a pact with the devil. At the front end, many who wielded Wylde Magick attempted to sever the pact. No one was ever able to break it."

Chloe's head snapped up. It was the first time she'd heard the term Wylde Magick. "Is that our brand of power?" she asked.

"Indeed." He nodded. "Wylde Magick on our side and Black or Dark Magick on the other."

"What you're saying is vampires are here to stay," Stephan spoke up. Sarai's uncle, he had her blond hair and blue eyes. A giant of a man and a mountain lion shifter, he'd been silent since Chloe sat down.

"I believe so," Zee replied. "And my dragon isn't contradicting me. Since we won't have much luck attacking things from the vampire end, our only other choice is dissuading mages from offering their magic."

"You wouldn't think it would be all that hard," Jeremiah muttered.

"Nay, you wouldn't," Niall agreed. "Yet here we are. Three more mages who offered up their bodies are now dead because of misplaced loyalties."

"Another complicating factor"—Chloe spread her

words out for emphasis—"is the residual antipathy betwixt shifters and mages."

"We can't solve everything," Zachary protested.

"Yes, but maybe that would be the best place to start," Chloe pressed.

"My sister makes a good point," Jeremiah said. "Mages signed on with vampires because of their hatred for shifters and the promises vamps made about annihilating us."

"Mmph. You didn't mention that earlier," Zee said. "Did you leave anything else out?"

"Who knows?" Sarai sounded irritated. She squeezed her eyes shut. "I'm tired. Can we continue this tomorrow?"

"We could, but I'm here now," Zee spoke up. "I'd like to get some proactive plans on the table, so we can pick the most promising ones to begin working on." He paused for a beat. "We need a solid offense."

"Agreed," Jeremiah said. "It's six. Let's break until seven and resume our strategy session. Between now and then"—he leveled his gaze at Zee—"come up with ideas for us to dissect."

"Deal." The dragon shifter rubbed his hands together. "If you would be so kind, I need at least four mages to shed light on your people. It would help tremendously."

"I'll volunteer," Jeremiah said. "My sister will as well. Beyond that, who else wants to be part of this?"

Raul and Johnny raised their hands. Everyone else walked out of the room. Chloe was delighted to be included, but she still didn't trust herself around the dragon shifter.

"Is there a smaller room we might retire to?" Zee asked. "Something more intimate, like a morning room or a parlor?"

The word intimate rolling from his mouth gave her chills. She wanted intimate from him all right, but she couldn't let him know how enticing she found him. They were comrades in arms. Nothing more. Nothing less. He hadn't given her the slightest indication he had any interest in her.

For all she knew, he might have a wife or multiple girlfriends stashed around Denver and points unknown.

"Sure. This way," Jeremiah was saying and led the way out of the dining room. Chloe figured he was heading toward the small parlor off the sunroom.

She waited until the men filed out before following them. Zee's enticing scent, heavy on heather this time, filled her nostrils, and she sucked air like a starving woman. By the time she walked into the snug parlor, she'd gotten herself more-or-less under control and picked a seat beneath the windows. It was perfect, far enough away from the dragon to maintain her composure.

She hoped.

Zee reached for her as she walked past, closing a warm, calloused hand around her arm. "Sit close, little mage. I promise I won't bite."

CHAPTER 3

Zee was a master at masking his reactions, but he'd had to exert effort not to show how shocked he was by the tale unfolding as variations emerged from both shifters and mages. Had they entered some latter-day phenomenon where magic's tenure on earth was drawing to a close?

Except vampires, that is. Those bleeding bastards would survive any Armageddon. Already being dead conferred interesting advantages. The cockroaches of the magical world, they'd still be hanging about chewing everyone else's remains, no matter what else happened.

The thought twisted his stomach into an unpleasantly tight knot. When Jeremiah suggested an hour's break, Zee glommed onto it as an opportunity for him to learn more about mages.

Not that he couldn't have dug information out of his extensive library and lore books, but this was faster.

The tall, statuesque blonde, Chloe, was avoiding him, but he'd be damned if he understood why. When she skittered past him, clearly intent on putting distance between them—again—he'd grabbed her arm. Maybe it was a bad idea, but he wasn't in the habit of second guessing his instincts.

"Sit close, little mage." He tried for a disarming smile. "I promise I won't bite."

She tugged out of his grasp and marched to a window seat upholstered in faded brocade. Color added definition to her high cheekbones. Once she was seated, she said, "Mages hold equal stature with shifters. I am not little."

"I'm sure he didn't mean anything by it. Don't be so touchy." Jeremiah was quick to step into the breach.

"Sorry," she mumbled and tucked her hands beneath her.

"It's fine." Zee selected an oversized chair covered in well-creased leather and eased into it. "I was out of line. Before you catch me up on mage history, do any of you have any idea why we suddenly ended up targeted by vampires? It can't be accidental they aimed their powers of coercion on mages. Do they know something we don't?"

"Not sure about that," Jeremiah replied, "but we're

at the tail end of a full set of twelve astrological ages, and—"

Zee felt like a fool. "Och. Say no more. I should have figured it out without being told." He started to say his dragon should have been on top of what was bound to be a period of paranormal unrest but criticizing his bondmate was a very bad idea. The last time he'd rebuked the dragon for handling something badly, the creature had wrested command of their shared body, taken to the skies, and annihilated a flock of sheep.

Back then, they flew far higher than arrows could reach, but the reality of a dragon scouring the countryside with fire had mobilized the clergy. The resultant witch hunt ended up with over a dozen magic-wielders swinging at the end of gibbets. The dragon hadn't apologized, but it hadn't pulled a similar stunt ever again, so some kind of lesson must have sunk in.

"According to Sarai"—Chloe untucked her hands from beneath her butt—"a plus from these magically unsettled times will be that many mages become shifters just like Jer did."

Zee remembered the wolf shifter dabbled in astrology and other psychic arts. She'd apparently been dredging through his chart, although where she'd unearthed precise data about his birth was a mystery

—unless she was the one who'd ended up with the missing lore books. A strong possibility since he'd been hunting for them since setting foot on American soil.

"Has that happened?" Zee asked. "Or is Jeremiah the only newly bonded shifter?"

"Not yet," Raul replied. "So far, Jer is the only one."

"There's not a mage walking who wouldn't welcome a bond animal," Johnny chimed in. Tall, slender, and dark-haired, he projected quiet competence.

"I've been trying," Chloe said. "Really hard. But no amount of magic seems to do the trick." The color across her delicately sculpted cheekbones deepened, so she was clearly embarrassed by her disclosure. "I figured since it was so easy for Jer, and he and I are twins, it would be simple enough for me to find my own bondmate..." Her voice ran down.

Zee wanted to comfort her, but she'd never accept anything from him. The straight set to her shoulders and spine revealed how proud she was. She'd rather die than let anyone coo over her.

Where before he'd felt a flash of attraction to her obvious beauty, now he was drawn to who she was. There was depth to the mage. Resilience and determination. All traits he admired.

He gazed around the small group in the parlor. "Are you the only mages not aligned with vampires?"

"Of course not," Raul replied. "We threw a wedding celebration for Niall and Sarai and Jeremiah and Renee a while back. Maybe three weeks ago. A couple dozen mages showed up and remained for hours, talking. They seemed to understand how vulnerable they were and agreed to make certain other mages warded themselves and were ultra-aware."

"Aye, so they wouldn't fall prey to crafty vampires on the prowl for their magic," Johnny put in.

Zee frowned. He didn't care for the sound of that, considering the three who'd shown up at the mages' house today. "Have you spoken with any of these ambassadors of goodwill since the mating ceremonies?"

"No," Jeremiah said. "What are you thinking?"

"That maybe they weren't what they appeared." He steepled his fingers in front of him. "Today proved vampires can masquerade as mages. Perhaps the contingent that showed up before were partially vampires." His mouth curved into a grim smile. "Wolves in sheep's clothing as it were."

"That's horrible." Chloe leapt from her chair and proceeded to pace around the room. "I've known all those mages my entire life. To think any of them would violate our hospitality like that turns my stomach."

"My people wouldn't resort to such tricks,"

Jeremiah ground out. "Your assertion is just one more example of residual antipathy between shifters and mages."

Zee furled his brows. "Today belies your statement." He didn't bother to mention he'd need to do some internal rearranging to cast shifters and mages as allies. He wasn't worried about the transition, but nor would it be automatic.

Jeremiah pinched the bridge of his nose between thumb and forefinger. When he looked at Zee, he said, "We can't trust anyone, huh?"

"Not unless you scan them with magic and come up with a clean bill of health," Zee agreed. He sat straighter. "I argued with my bondmate earlier today, told it that its assessment of how bad things are was overdrawn. I no longer feel that way."

Chloe came to a halt in front of her brother. "We have to check on Curt and Viva. Alexander Westerly too, and all the rest of them. They may be in trouble. They might need us. They—"

Jeremiah made a chopping motion. "Stand down, sister. We will do what we can, but we're not walking into a trap. Perhaps that was the underlying rationale behind today. Vampires assumed we'd be furious at how they used our kin, worried sick about the other mages, and walk right into an ambush."

Zee offered Jeremiah points for clear thinking. It

was the same conclusion he'd already drawn. "Sound logic," he growled. "Vampires have always had a high tolerance for collateral damage. I suppose it's a consequence of already being dead. If they thought sacrificing three of their number would bring fresh magic within easy reach, they'd have made the exchange without thinking about it."

"It's almost seven," Jeremiah pointed out. "Are you missing anything elemental before we reconvene with everyone else?"

Zee shook his head. "I have many of the old lore books—"

"Sarai does as well," Chloe cut in.

"Good to know. I'm certain I can fill in any blanks between her library and my own." Zee stopped short of saying something to the effect of, 'so that's where they went.' He'd sought the misplaced volumes for years. Not so much because he was interested in their wisdom but because anything incomplete needled him.

Jeremiah stood. "See you in the dining room."

Zee rose as well. "Give me a few minutes. There's a matter I would converse with my dragon about."

"Of course." Jeremiah strode from the room with Raul and Johnny close behind him. Chloe gave him a wide berth as she darted through the door, but he didn't call her back or comment as he had when they entered the small parlor.

As soon as the others were gone, he pushed the door shut with a jot of magic and turned his attention inward. *"How complicated would it be to find bond animals for this group?"*

"Why ask me?" the dragon countered.

"You're the one with the connection to the animals' world." Zee didn't bother with telepathy this time. If anyone stood on the far side of the door, he'd have sensed them with magic, and the carpeted hall was empty.

"I could ask around," the dragon hedged.

"You're dodging my question."

"Not exactly." The dragon's voice took on a querulous note. *"Only some of these mages are worthy of the shifter bond."*

"And you've determined this, how? We've spent all of a couple of hours here." His voice had risen, and he made a grab for his temper. He'd always been quick to anger; his long association with the dragon hadn't mitigated that tendency one whit.

"You will not question me." The dragon moved from querulous to imperious.

Zee switched tactics. "For the ones you deem worthy, how can we hasten the bonding process?"

Steam billowed from his mouth, followed by smoke. Zee hastily crossed the room and pushed a window open, grateful when the sash lifted and caught, remaining open.

"I must discuss this with the animals' council."

A gout of flame followed the smoke, but Zee had anticipated as much, and it blasted harmlessly out the window. By the time he made certain none of the wet greenery outside was in danger of turning into the next burning bush, the dragon was gone.

He shut the window after inhaling a deep lungful of icy air. Why was he hurrying what was looking like an inevitable process? If one mage turned shifter, doubtless others would as well. They had sufficient magic to support such a transformation. Sarai may have stolen books rightfully his, but her interpretations had always been spot on. If she said mages were about to turn into shifters, he believed her. They'd been a unified people once, so it wasn't a quantum leap for it to happen again.

Zee cringed. He'd sent his dragon off in search of prospective candidates because he wanted Chloe to be so overcome with gratitude, she'd grace his bed with her lissome, six-foot gorgeousness. Or maybe she'd accept an offer to ride him when he was in dragon form.

The thought brought his cock shooting to attention. He groaned and pushed it to a less noticeable position. Not now. This was not a time to lose himself in a planned seduction. He needed all his faculties to address the problem at hand. Having more shifters would be a great help dealing with vampires.

If Chloe were a shifter, she'd be a better soldier. End of story. Besides, nowhere existed for him to fly free with her astride him. Someone would see, take a picture with their cellphone, and plaster it all over the Internet. He supposed he could spirt her off somewhere in the dead of night, cloak them with strong spells, and...

He ground his teeth. Some aspects of living in the twenty-first century rankled, and the almost total lack of privacy sat at the top of the list. What the hell was wrong with people and their endless selfies—and the self-absorption that went along with them?

He redirected himself to the problem at hand.

Since mages were the ones bound by mesmerism, it followed the more of them who became shifters, the stronger an army they'd have. He sent good thoughts after the dragon but decided to keep his mouth shut until he heard back from his bondmate.

No point in getting anyone's hopes up, only to have them dashed.

There was still the problem of the mages the dragon deemed "unworthy." Zee rolled his mental eyes. He hadn't picked up on any lesser mages in the house. Some were quieter than others, but all of them had been outraged by today's attack and willing to do whatever was needed to avoid a repeat of allowing vampires to cross their lintel.

A knock on the door snapped his head up. "Hey, mate," Niall called through the door. "You coming? We're all waiting on you."

Zee crossed the room and pulled the door open. "Sorry. The dragon isn't always as tractable as I'd like."

Niall snaked a thread of magic outward until it wrapped around Zee. "Hmmm. It appears you sent your bondmate on an errand. What was it?"

"You know me too well."

Niall shrugged. "'Twas a time when I did, but you didn't answer my question."

Zee reached around the jaguar shifter and pushed the door shut. "I'm trying to circumvent the time factor."

"Eh? You're talking in riddles, but then you always did."

"No. You're not listening." Zee smothered annoyance. "Look. Bond animals take their sweet time selecting us. I was simply trying to shorten the timeline. I sent the dragon to the animals' world to locate potential bond animals. The more mages who become shifters, the—"

Niall punched him in the arm. "Brilliant. I get it.

Sure and 'tis a grand idea. How long before dragon-boy returns?"

Zee winced. "Never, never let it hear you call it that. You'll end up a pile of scorched cinders. And I have no idea how long before my bondmate will return. Probably hours rather than days, though."

He directed magic to open the door. "Keep your mouth shut."

"Of course. No reason to get everyone's hopes up."

Niall's words mirrored Zee's earlier thoughts. He didn't bother to correct the jaguar about "everyone." That was a battle he'd fight once the dragon returned. He followed Niall to the dining room. Someone had lit sconces, bathing the room in a warm, golden glow. Platters laden with bread, sliced meat, and cut-up vegetables sat on a sideboard. He filled a plate before grabbing an empty seat.

After a few minutes where no one said much, Zee understood it had to be because no one knew quite what to do next. It was one thing to craft a defense and wait for the mage-magic-fueled vampires to show up. Quite another to go on the offensive.

He looked across the table at Sarai. "I understand you have some lore books."

She nodded. "Yup. That I do. Far from a full set, but no one else wanted them, so they ended up with me."

Hot words about her stealing them out from under him once they landed in New York wanted out. He forced them back. They'd accomplish nothing beyond turning her and Niall into enemies. Holding a neutral expression, he said, "I have the rest of them. As a first step, I say we reunite the library. Those old books hold power. Together, they'll yield answers if we're persistent."

She rested her chin on an upraised hand, regarding him. "You may be right. Bring what you have to my shop in downtown Denver. Once they're there, we can work with them."

Zee smiled to himself. Sarai was just as protective of her books as he was of his collection, but the ancient tomes and scrolls had that effect on their caretakers. It ensured their survival.

"Might be simpler to transport yours to my home," he said smoothly. "I'm sure it's larger and more commodious than your shop."

Sarai bristled. "Look, Mr. Famous Judge—"

"I was not casting aspersions on your place of business," he broke in. "My home is well-warded, off the beaten track, and we're unlikely to be disturbed. If your shop holds the same benefits, I'm fine with meeting there."

"He has a point, niece," Stephan said. "Any more

than half a dozen people in your shop, and there's barely space to breathe."

Zee's next concession came hard, but he dove into it, willing to go the extra mile. He wanted the rest of his books, but Sarai would be more willing to agree if he offered assurances.

He pushed his plate off to one side and splayed his hands on the table. "I'd be a liar if I didn't admit to hunting for the books that are companions to mine, but you have my word I will not attempt to hold onto the volumes you bring into my home. Once we're done, you're free to sequester them as you choose."

"Deal." Sarai leaned across the table, hand extended. Zee clasped it. A short, hot blast of power hit him square in the chest as she tested his intentions.

"Goddammit, woman," he sputtered. "You have to stop tossing truth spells about. I'm on your side. Either accept it, or I'll be on my way."

He felt Chloe's gaze on him but kept his eyes firmly on Sarai. Truth time. Either he was part of this group. Or not. If they booted him, he'd continue to work on the problem, but no need to spell that out. He'd always been a party of one, preferred things that way.

Sarai nodded once, her shrewd gaze boring into him. "It goes against the grain, but I'll do my best to trust you're in this for the common good."

"Thank you." Zachary recognized opportunity when it showed up. If they somehow came out on top of things, he would have reinstated himself with his kinsfolks. It was worth the hardship of decisions by committee. One of the best things about being a judge was it was his show. He did his research, promulgated opinions, and no one questioned them. Unless a disgruntled defendant dragged his case to a higher court, which didn't happen often.

He stood. "I'll head home and be ready when you show up."

"I can't teleport with that many books," Sarai pointed out.

"We'll stop by Stephan's first and collect a car," Niall said, "although I don't care for the idea of us splitting up."

"I'm coming with you," Stephan growled. "We can take the truck."

"Should be all right," Raul said brusquely. "Vampires require an invitation, and we'll keep the castle gates barred till you return."

Chloe got to her feet. "No easy way to say this"— her gaze fell on her twin before scuttling away—"but I have a few books too."

"What?" Jeremiah looked thunderstruck. "From where?"

"It's a long story, but the short version is you

wondered why I knew where Mitch was holed up. Not sure how much you recall, but he fancied himself quite the seer. I learned a few castings from him, but my reason for returning there was I wanted his source materials."

Her nostrils flared, and she looked down. "One day I showed up, and no one was home. I figured the goddess had cleared the decks for me to make my move, so I took the books and ran. Tried teleporting, but didn't get more than a few feet, so I hiked out of there. It was really hard because I had to hide myself and my trail with magic. Didn't want Mitch coming after me. Took two days until I reached a road and stuck out my thumb."

"You stole from Mitch?" Jeremiah's tone held a dangerous undercurrent.

Chloe glanced up. "Aye, and a good thing too, wouldn't you say? Had he hung onto our magical tomes, they'd now be in vampire hands."

"You didn't know that at the time. Christ, Chloe." Jeremiah set his mouth in a harsh line. "I thought I knew you."

"All's well that ends well," Zee cut in, anxious to smooth things over—and leverage the opportunity her disclosure presented. "By all means, please bring your magical accoutrements to my home as well. Since our power springs from common roots, it's quite possible your volumes will complement ours."

"We could wait until the morrow," Niall said.

"No." Sarai's response was firm. "We need to move on this." She creased her forehead in thought. "Let's see. We'll teleport home, drive to my shop, collect the books, and—"

Zee rattled off an address and added a telepathic image. "I'll have coffee ready. My bet is you'll show up in a couple of hours."

"I'll go with Sarai, Niall, and Stephan. Give me a moment to gather my things." Chloe turned to leave.

"Don't be ridiculous," Zee said. "You'll come with me. It's far more straightforward since I have more than enough magic to teleport with inanimate objects in tow."

"We can too," Sarai countered. "Just not armloads of them."

Chloe turned slowly. "I don't think it's a good idea."

He walked across the room until he faced her squarely. "Same thing I said to Sarai goes for you and everyone here. Either you trust I'm one of you. Or not. If it's the latter, I'll be on my way."

He met Chloe's forthright blue gaze head on. She was shorter than him, but only by a couple of inches.

"Good point. Wait a moment while I collect the books and my bag."

Niall, Sarai, and Stephan had moved to the far end of the room. Power boiled around them, turning the air thick and shiny. Moments later, they were gone. Zee waited for Jeremiah to blast upright and say Chloe required a chaperone, but it didn't happen. The cave lion shifter sat unmoving, jaws clenched. Clearly, he was still unnerved by his twin's disclosure. Renee gripped his clasped hands, offering silent support.

Zee strode through the room. Before he walked out the door, he turned and said, "If anything appears the least bit out of place, summon me with telepathy, and I'll return instantly. Vampire coercion has no effect on me."

"How about their venom?" Jeremiah glanced up.

"Now that would be a problem." Zee grinned. "Just need to make certain I don't stand still long enough for them to sink their fangs into me."

He ducked through the door and into the hallway as Chloe rattled down a staircase, a leather bag hanging off one shoulder and her arms filled with books. He didn't offer to take any of them. She'd be loathe to let them go, and his mission was to create trust, not shatter it.

"Ready?"

At her curt nod, he drew power and whisked them

away determined to be so damned proper, the Queen of the Fae couldn't find fault with his deportment. He was delighted by the turn of events that had thrown him and Chloe together, but she was still skittish as a young colt.

Lots of sugar was the key here. And a paddock with the gate left open.

CHAPTER 4

Chloe clutched the armload of leather-bound volumes. They were heavy, but she'd be damned if she'd ask for help. For whatever reason, Zee hadn't offered any. Maybe this would turn out better than it had begun. Jeremiah was furious with her. She knew him inside out, and the rigid set of his shoulders never boded well. They'd have more words about her actions.

She expected the travel spell to last for at least a short time, but less than five minutes elapsed before the blackness ceded to gray. The outlines of an enormous house came into view as Zee brought them out in an extravagant garden sprawling before his front door.

Chloe gazed from one end of the manicured flowering hedges to the other and grinned despite herself. "Magic, eh?"

He shrugged, eyes glinting with amusement. "What else? Not much blooms late in the year without some kind of an assist. I thought you might be more comfortable if you started in the gardens and could see the house from the outside."

She offered him credit for trying to put her at ease. "It's lovely. A veritable retreat."

"That's how I've always viewed it. I had my eye on this piece of property for a long time. The second it came on the market, I made certain they'd accept my offer and no other."

She quirked a brow. "More magic?"

He grinned, looking like a mischievous boy, and she quashed an almost overwhelming hunger to thread her fingers through his hair. "I'll never tell. Come on inside. I bet you'd love to set those books down."

She followed him up broad, flagstone steps. The house was a combination of wood, glass, and stone. Four floors showed above ground, with a line of windows suggesting a subterranean basement. Double oak doors inscribed with runes swung open. Perhaps they sensed their master's presence because she hadn't felt any magic.

"Surely those doors weren't here before," she observed.

"Aye, they were, but I may have embellished them a wee bit with carvings."

"I bet the runes serve a purpose."

He turned an approving glance her way. "Smart, wench. They make it simpler to keep my home warded."

"We haven't been referred to as wenches since the nineteenth century." Chloe tried for indignation but couldn't make it past amusement.

He snorted. "Och, lassie. My roots just bled through. Can ye ever forgive me?"

His brogue had turned thick as clotted cream, and she gave up on smothering the smile that wanted out. "Not sure. I'll work on it, though."

"Excellent. I really am a likeable fellow given half a chance."

Chloe didn't point out he was far too self-assured for likeable to fit. As a Leo with her Leo twin, she knew all about egos clashing, about not bothering to establish consensus, about knowing to her bones a particular decision was right.

Like the one where she'd filched the magical tomes tucked in her arms from Mitch. Not that Jeremiah might not have agreed with her actions—if he'd been part of the initial planning. He didn't like being broadsided, took it as an affront. Zee was like Jer—and like her. He grabbed the point and ran with his instincts.

Thinking about how commanding he was, how

confident, heated her blood. Most men didn't appeal to her, but this one did.

Zee had moved through the door, so she walked inside, taking in polished wooden floors covered with silken rugs worked into Oriental designs. Heavy old furniture was tastefully arranged into conversation groups. One large room extended at least fifty feet in front of her. A floor to ceiling fireplace made of stone sat at the end. Crystal and silver antiques graced the room's many tables. Bronze carvings depicting shifters in the midst of changing form stood in each corner. The effect was understated, tasteful wealth.

Zee barked a word, and the fire crackled to life. "Feel like sitting by the hearth?" he asked. "You can settle in while I start a pot of coffee and see what nourishment I can offer the others when they show up."

Chloe strolled closer to the fire and placed her books and shoulder bag on a small padded divan. Fragrant smoke curled up the chimney. "Need any help?" she inquired, and then kicked herself. She'd offered because she wanted to remain by his side. Not a good reason at all, and one she needed to divest herself of fast.

"No. I'll be fine."

It wasn't the answer she'd expected, but she took the rebuff in stride and focused on the flickering flames. He loped easily across the great room, disappearing through an archway on one side. Once he was gone, she lectured herself.

He's a shifter. A dragon shifter. He sits at the top of the shifter hierarchy, except maybe for Jer's cave lion. Regardless, he could have his choice of appropriate mates. Shifter women. But he appears to be single. Maybe he likes it that way. Some men hate being tied down.

Beyond his marital preferences, I bet anything he sees mage magic as inferior, just like Niall and them did when they first met us.

She sat next to her books and opened one on her lap. She hadn't spent much time with this particular tome. Maybe it held the secret to the bondmate she longed for. Closing her eyes, she drew magic and asked it the same question she'd asked the other books.

"How can I find my bondmate?"

To her surprise, pages riffled. Before when she'd asked the question, the books had remained inert in her hands. Pages were still flipping when Zachary walked back into the room. He'd changed out of his suit into dark slacks and a cream-colored shirt that set off his shapely shoulders. A gold and silver pendant of a dragon in flight hung from his neck on a thick golden chain.

He settled across from her. "Find anything?"

She shook her head. "The book is still working."

"What did you ask?" He arched a red brow.

"Hush. You're interrupting my concentration." Indeed, the pages had slowed to a crawl. Either the answer was about to reveal itself, or her efforts had come to naught. The book quieted. When she glanced down, the pages were blank. Disappointment arrowed through her, bitter and bleak.

Angry words crowded at the back of her throat. She'd been close, but his presence derailed her casting. Before something she regretted leaked out, he moved nearer, crouching so he could see the book too. He trailed fingertips down the blank page and runes came into view. At first, they spun like little tops, but then they fell into rows like obedient soldiers.

"How did you do that?" she demanded.

He shrugged. "Magical things like me."

She choked down an angry retort because his statement implied they didn't care much for her. Instead, she focused on the runes. Ancient Gaelic. She could read it, but it would be a slog. Undeterred, she started with the first line.

Obviously, he wasn't plagued by her lack of language skills because he said, "You're a single-minded one, eh?"

She pursed her lips into a straight line and flicked a

finger at the creased vellum page. "I suppose you can read this?"

"Easily. You're still seeking magic that will net you a bondmate." He pulled the book off her lap and closed it, laying it on the floor.

"What are you doing? Give it back. I was closer than I've—"

"Nay, lassie." The brogue was back. "Ye werena close at all. 'Tisn't how this works. Ye canna magic-up a bondmate. They must select you. Once that happens, ye open yourself to the magic and voila."

"But I've waited and waited—" She cut her words off at the source. She sounded like a whiny ten-year-old. "Never mind." Being this close to him was doing odd things to her mind. Or maybe it was the power emanating from his pendant. The golden ornament pulsed with enchantment.

Chloe stumbled to her feet and took two steps until she stood in front of the fire. Mercifully, he didn't follow her.

"I know what it is to want and be disappointed," he said, his voice low and vibrating with an emotion she had no name for.

To deflect his attention away from her pathetic attempts to find a bondmate, she asked, "What kind of things do you want? From the looks of your home, you lack for nothing."

"I would go back in time, return to the Old Country where magic was revered. I would fly free." His voice rose. "I'm a dragon, a mythical beast in today's world. Do you have any idea what that means?"

She turned and faced him where he still knelt on the floor. "Magic wasn't all that revered. We fled your precious Old Country because clerics were burning and hanging us. I bet you weren't doing much flying then, either. Naught that would reveal what you truly were."

He looked shocked, as if she'd slapped him. "I was referring to a time before magic fell out of fashion. You may not be old enough to remember when mankind worshipped us."

A corner of her mouth curled downward. "Did they sacrifice virgins to you?" She'd meant to be funny, edged with sarcasm, but he surged to his feet.

"Do not mock me, mage. Magic is serious business. My bond animal is a gift. One you long for."

She squared her shoulders. "You don't intimidate me. Your magic doesn't, either. Yeah, I want a bondmate, but if I was bonded, I wouldn't turn into an arrogant dick."

His face darkened, eyebrows drawing into a single menacing line. "Show some respect." Steam blasted from his mouth, bathing her in heat.

"I will when you do." She couldn't have ripped her

gaze from him if she'd tried. Damn, he was even more appealing angry. She balanced on the balls of her feet, ready for anything. Part of her wished Sarai and the others would show up. A much bigger part hoped they'd stay gone forever.

With no warning, the room shaded to mist. She warded herself. What the hell was going on? Had the dragon shifter done something? Imprisoned her? It felt like she'd slipped into another world. The air thickened and turned into a bevy of colors, heavy on blues and violets. Smells buffeted her, wild things romping through cold, damp moors. She turned in a circle, hands extended, but couldn't determine where she was.

Should she try to claw her way back to the place she'd left? A quick assessment exposed curiosity and fascination. She wasn't afraid, though she ought to be. Whatever had yanked her through a portal into another world was incredibly powerful. She'd do well to be terrified of it, yet nothing around her felt threatening.

Chloe dropped her hands to her sides and stood tall. "Who are you, and why am I here?" She released her wards, determined to get to the bottom of this.

"Aha! So you want me after all. Those incantations and tears were real."

"Of course they were, but which ones are you

referring to?" She narrowed her eyes, trying to peer through the mist. Did Zee think she'd cried over him? How could he possibly be so conceited? Hell, she barely knew him. Still, it had to be him talking to her. No one else was here.

Gleaming shrouds shimmered and thinned. An impossibly large red dragon, forelegs folded over its scaled chest, regarded her squarely through whirling silver eyes. "*I have chosen you, mage. Accept the bond, or it is my right to slay you where you stand.*"

Chloe blinked hard. The dragon had to be chimera, an imaginary figment mocking her. "A dragon?" she stuttered. "But I assumed, or I thought... Nah, you can't be real."

The dragon opened its mouth. Fire blasted out. Some caught the edges of her jacket, and the fabric began to smolder. Chloe batted at the flames. They were real enough, so maybe the dragon was too.

Wonder began in the soles of her feet and swept through her until she was giddy. Her longstanding dream stood before her. Not that she'd ever fantasized a dragon bondmate, but this might be better than her most fervent imaginings.

"*What?*" the creature watched her. "*Would you have preferred something soft and fluffy? Sorry. The bond doesn't work that way. I am here. You must choose.*"

Chloe's heart cracked open. It was finally happening. So what if she'd never envisioned a dragon bondmate? The scaled giant towering above her was gorgeous, if a bit intimidating. She took a step toward it. "All the years I longed for a bondmate, I said I would be happy with any animal. It never occurred to me someone as powerful as yourself would be interested in me, but I'm grateful." She choked on words, throat thick with emotion. "So grateful."

A tear tracked down her cheek, mostly because she still couldn't believe her fondest wish was finally coming true.

The dragon puffed more steam. *"Open yourself to my form. This will hurt the first time. More pain than you've ever imagined, but it will get easier."*

"I'm ready."

"Nay, you're not. Remove your clothes. Unless you don't care about being naked once you find your body again."

For one wild moment, she wondered if this wasn't an illusion, crafted by Zee, to get her into bed, and then she buried the thought ten feet under and scrambled out of her clothes. She had to assume this was really happening. She didn't sense Zachary anywhere, and she wanted the dragon to respect her, view her as worthy.

Perhaps it already did, since it had chosen her, but

she could ruin everything if she wasn't careful. Chloe stepped away from her clothing.

The dragon nodded and unfolded its forelegs. *"Listen carefully. You shall take my form, and then we will fly, but not for long. Your magic must grow—a lot. If you spend too much time as a dragon, it will drain you quickly, and your magic is needed to fight vampires."*

"Where are we?" She stepped nearer the dragon to take advantage of heat emanating from its hide.

"A borderworld. You can fly without fear of discovery or retribution from puny men who are frightened of anything they can't explain away with science."

She inhaled nervously. She'd stumbled onto borderworlds before, and nearly been lost. Finding her way back had taken gargantuan effort and a clear head, but that task was in the future. The prospect of flight, of being a dragon, made her dizzy with anticipation.

"I'm ready," she repeated and licked at dry lips.

"Open your magical center. No matter what happens, do not close it."

Fear battled hope. What if this was a sophisticated trap? What if the minute she left herself vulnerable, a vampire swooped in and snared her?

"Believe, little mage, or we cannot proceed." The dragon's voice was unexpectedly supportive, a far cry

from when it threatened to kill her if she refused the bond.

Chloe nodded. Belief was the cornerstone of everything magical. Why should this be any different? You pictured the magic working, and then it did. She stared straight into the dragon's whirling eyes. Silvery pools, they sucked her into their depths. Next, she opened herself to the creature from legend and visualized joining with it. Her heart pounded, and her mouth was dry, but she didn't back down.

"Excellent." Fire swooshed from the dragon.

Its edges blurred—or maybe it was her vision. Something sharp sliced through an arm, then a leg. The invisible blade scored her back, her ribs, her shoulders, but the hot gush of blood never came. She ground her teeth, determined to be strong, to not cry out as her entire existence turned into tortured anguish. The dragon had warned her, but pain wasn't the type of thing you could prepare for. It was always worse than you imagined it would be.

The world tilted on its axis. Bones cracked and stretched. Skin yielded to scales. Wings sprouted in twin points of liquid agony as they pierced her shoulder blades. Her arms shortened. Her legs grew thick. Brilliant red talons shot from the ends of her feet and hands.

She gasped for breath, amazed as her new lung

configuration took in air, trading it for smoke, steam, and fire. When the first gout of fire rolled from her mouth, she jumped back, terrified it would burn her. The throbbing, stinging, aching, stabbing, gnarly pain was lessening, not by much, but any decrease was a victory.

"You're past the crux point. Spread those wings." The dragon's voice reverberated through her head. *"Go ahead. Don't be afraid. We were born to fly."*

Chloe extended first one wing, and then the other. The anguish that had overshadowed everything fell away, not totally gone but almost. She moved her wings up and down—and remained firmly glued to earth. What was she doing wrong? Born to fly didn't match up with her useless flapping.

"Walk forward," the dragon instructed.

Chloe did and almost fell off the edge of a sharp cliff. *"Whoa."* She stumbled back a step, clumsy on ungainly back legs.

"Whoa, my ass," the dragon retorted. *"Step off the cliff."*

"But we'll fall."

"You've trusted me this far."

So she had. Chloe eyed the thousands of feet stretching below the edge of the cliff. Borderworlds housed strange things. What was waiting for her at the bottom?

"You'll never find out," the dragon said acidly.

"You read my mind."

"That and other things. Now get moving."

Something akin to a whip crashed across her back, and Chloe sprang forward, spreading her wings as soon as the dirt beneath her rear feet crumbled away. She flapped frantically, expecting nothing, and was filled with relief when her body, so large, awkward, and cumbersome on land, became easy to manage. The wings she hadn't trusted held her suspended in the air. She flew first one way, and then another, delighted with maneuvering in three dimensions rather than two.

"See?" The dragon apparently couldn't resist an I-told-you-so moment.

Chloe swooped. She banked. She did an aerial flip. The last delighted her so much, she belched fire. *"I love this."* She bugled her delight to the skies of the borderworld, and they developed gilt edges in response to her glee.

Chloe sobered. *"Thank you. You've given me an incredible gift. One I've longed for all my life, but the reality exceeds my expectations a million times over."*

"Only a million?"

Chloe started to answer but realized her bondmate was teasing her.

After a few more aerial cartwheels, the dragon said, *"Time to go back. Your kinfolks need you."*

She wheeled and headed for her stack of clothing. *"Why couldn't I fly from the spot where I tried the first time?"*

"It's like anything else new, an assist makes all the difference. Nothing like heaps of open air to ease into being a dragon."

Chloe landed next to her clothes and girded herself for agony. *"Tell me how to find my body."*

"Good. You're coming to trust me. Trust is our foundation, our bedrock. It's the one element that must always sit betwixt you and me."

Chloe waited, but the dragon didn't say anything further. She opened her magical center wider and held an image of herself as human. The same process that had flayed skin from bone happened in reverse, except this time the discomfort was far more manageable.

She shrugged into her clothes, bending to tie her bootlaces. The task she'd feared—leaving the borderworld—loomed before her. "How do I get back?" she asked.

"How do you think? If you'd come here by yourself, what would you do?"

Chloe squared her shoulders and summoned power. It jumped to her call, far more potent than she remembered it, and she blessed the dragon for sharing its magic. Balancing energy between her hands, she visualized Zee's living room. What would he think about her new affiliation? Would he be thrilled or see her as an interloper?

Guess I'm about to find out.

She sent her power outward, riding on its coattails. The borderworld shimmered into nothingness, replaced by the stark grace of Zachary's great room. She was gathering her wits, solidifying her transition from one world to the other, when arms closed around her from behind and Zee's unmistakable scent enveloped her.

Heather, gorse, and lilacs thickened, and she gulped air like a starving woman. He held her tight before turning her in her arms and gazing into her eyes. "Thank all the gods you're unharmed. I would have gone after you, but my dragon held me back. It spoke true. The path you trod had no space for me."

It took a moment before his words sank in. "You know, then?"

His mouth curved into a pleased smile. "Indeed, I do. And I welcome the first new dragon shifter in three hundred years." He kissed her forehead, and she turned her face upward, hoping for a real kiss. Instead, he went on, "I can't wait to fly with you. We'll figure something out. Find a way where we don't reveal what we are."

Something he'd said earlier didn't jive. She reared back enough to look at him. "If you knew I was finding my bondmate, why were you worried about me?"

"Och, lassie." He morphed into Gaelic. "So much could have gone wrong. 'Tis a hard transition. Ye might not have lived through it, especially not at your age. Why do ye think so few of us exist?"

She remembered the pain, how it surrounded her, attacked her, bit and excoriated every inch of her naked body.

His gaze never left her face. "Aye, the transition from skin to scales is a rocky one. Thanks be to all the gods, it gets easier."

"Same thing my dragon said." Pride cascaded through her at the words, *my dragon*. They sounded so right, but pretentious too.

A sharp blast of shifter magic buffeted her just before a portal formed, admitting Sarai, Niall, and Stephan. They'd split up the books, each of them carrying some. "Sorry it took so long." Stephan held a haggard look. He snapped off a word in Gaelic, and the portal turned to a fine mist before vanishing entirely.

"Aye. Fucking vampires thought to waylay us. Luckily, I had the foresight to bring a blade along." Niall puffed out a terse breath. "Bollocks. I need a drink."

"Of course." Zee let go of Chloe and walked to a mirrored sideboard. He pulled the doors open and said, "Help yourself."

"After the vamps, it didn't seem prudent to burn up time driving," Stephan went on, "so we took as many books as we could teleport with. A few remain in Sarai's shop."

Sarai had pinned a pointed look on Chloe and raised a red brow. "Getting cozy, were you?" The wolf shifter's gaze sharpened. "Something is different."

Magic zinged around Chloe before she could evade it.

Sarai's blue eyes widened, and she shrieked. "I knew it," just before she set her books on a side table, hurried to Chloe, and hugged her.

"Knew what, darling?" Niall asked from where he was pouring something that smelled like whiskey into a cut-crystal tumbler.

"If you weren't so rummy from killing vampires, you'd have noticed." Sarai was still hugging Chloe tight. "She's a shifter now, just like us."

Niall whistled.

Stephan trotted close and clapped Chloe on the back. "Congratulations, sister. Which animal selected you?"

Chloe extricated herself from Sarai's arms. Her

face heated under everyone's scrutiny, but she held herself proud. "My bondmate is a dragon. A beautiful red dragon with silver eyes."

Too overcome by emotion to say anything else, she felt her eyes fill with tears.

An Hour Earlier

Zachary sprang from where he'd been crouched on the floor. He and Chloe had exchanged heated words, but he'd scarcely expected magic to invade his home—his warded home—and make off with her. He stared at the spot she'd been sucked into the ether and hastily pulled magic, intent on going after her.

She'd stood up to him, maintained her dignity. Her refusal to back down under his censure made her incredibly appealing to him. He bet she'd be a spitfire in bed, but that was a topic to visit another day. First, he had to find her, bring her back.

Och, I can save her. She'll be so grateful, the rest will follow as night does day.

The Sir Galahad part of his nature liked the idea.

He'd been raised in an era where women deferred to men, were appreciative and appropriately thankful when a knight came to their rescue.

Power built around him. Should be simple enough to track her. She only had a few moments' head start. He laid markers in his great room. They'd draw him back in case he lost track of where he was. Humans had no idea their puny little Earth was but a single cog in a much larger wheel. Hundreds of borderworlds were spread through this galaxy and others.

He waited, willing his travel spell to reach maximum velocity.

The dragon blasted into his mind. *"You are not leaving this room."*

Zee rolled his shoulders back and hung onto his power. "And why not? Chloe needs me. She was here a moment ago, and—"

"I know precisely where she was. I also know where she is now." The dragon paused. It adored drama.

Zee could have throttled it. "Are you planning to tell me?"

"Not in so many words. I did as you requested, rustled up a few animals that weren't opposed to forming bonds."

The power bubbling around Zee had a bite to it, and his skin prickled. The dragon had been crystal clear they weren't going anywhere. He could get into a pitched battle with his bondmate, one he might not win depending on how intransigent the dragon chose to be, or he could capitulate. At least, for now.

Depending on how things rolled out, he could recreate his casting.

Only problem was Chloe's trail would be much colder then.

He released his travel spell and turned his attention inward. "All right," he told the dragon. "Thank you for helping scare up potential bondmates. Since you knew where Chloe was, why not have her prospective bond animal come here? It's as safe as anywhere these days."

Smoke billowed into Zee's mouth; he opened it, puffing out little gray rings. *"You already know the answer,"* the dragon countered. *"You're not thinking."*

Possibilities battered him as he ran through every bond animal until the obvious smacked him between the eyes. "Arrgh. Christ on a cross. She's bonding with a dragon?" Zee spat out smoke and steam, choking on them. His breath came hard through the narrow place his throat had become, and he splatted power in a circle, hastily resurrecting his spell.

"I have to go to her. She needs me. It's rough, that first transition. She might die."

"Stand down." The dragon inserted its essence between Zee and his magic.

It shocked him. The creature had never done that before. "Move aside," he ordered in a terse tone, fully prepared to engage his bondmate in battle.

"When did your faith waver?" the dragon asked.

"The last dragon shifter bonded three hundred twenty-six years ago. That's when. Others have accepted dragons, but they died during their first shift." He ground his jaws so hard, he was surprised his teeth didn't crack. "You know all this. Since the last pair of shifters lost their lives, no one has accepted a dragon's offer."

"And that is about to change, if it hasn't already." The dragon had retreated to its insufferably smug tone.

"How can you know?"

"Your lack of trust in me is disturbing." Fire shot from Zee's mouth. Apparently, the dragon was done with smoke.

"This has naught to do with you—" Zee began.

"It has everything to do with me," the dragon thundered. *"Do you believe dragons have been satisfied with the status quo? We've been relegated not to the extinct, but to the mythical. We are real, goddess be damned. Real. Do you hear me?"*

The small flame had turned to an inferno. Zee twisted so the fire spewing from him could join flames shooting up the chimney.

"*I hand-picked a bondmate for Chloe,*" the dragon went on, still screaming as fire blasted from Zachary.

"I'm sure you did," Zee managed in the lull between flames. "But this isn't about the dragon. It's about how strong Chloe is." He crouched to make it easier for his fire to join the one already burning.

Something hot and harsh fell across his back. Lashes from the dragon's tail. Once. Twice. Three times. "Stop it." He splayed his hands on the hearth, determined not to fall on his ass.

"*Listen and listen good,*" the dragon snarled. "*Shifters are not all the same. Neither are dragons. 'Tis the combination that makes for a successful bond.*" Its voice softened, but not by much. "*Magic has been fading. This last astrological age has been very hard on it. Why do you think mankind stopped believing in the supernatural? Nor is it accidental shifters and mages ended up in a war where many on both sides perished.*"

"Those ages last something like two thousand years, right?"

"*Closer to three, but you've missed the point as you often do.*"

Zee winced but didn't come up with a snappy retort. "Magic is weaker, I agree." Puzzle pieces clicked into place. He didn't like the result, but it stared back at him anyway.

"*Say it,*" the dragon urged.

"Shifters no longer command sufficient magic to survive the transition to dragon, and dragons aren't strong enough to pull them through the rough spots. Bonding with other animals is still possible, but that's not what's at stake here." Concern for Chloe returned in a rush. "If all that's true, Chloe needs me. Why did you hold me back? I could have lent my power, ensured a successful shift."

"Really? And how would that work?"

No longer playing host to uncontrolled dragon fire, Zachary straightened. It pained him to admit it, but his bondmate was right. A shifter's initiation was a very small island, one built just for two. His magic would only muck things up, and Chloe's dragon would take his intrusion as an affront.

"Finally. Thinking and not reacting," the dragon inserted. *"The wyrm I selected for your female mage is one I've known forever."*

"Of course you have," Zee muttered. "All of you know each other. There haven't been any new dragons in eons."

"As I was saying," his bondmate went on, *"this dragon would be outraged—and hurt—by your need to poke your oar into its fledgling bond. Trust it will pull Chloe through the worst of the first shift."*

Pain shot up his arms, and he unclenched hands he'd balled into tight fists. Whether he'd been frantic to quell the fire, or his unease, was hard to sort out. He paced from one end of the great room to the other and then back again. He was a take-charge kind of guy. Sitting back while things beyond his control played out grated.

More than grated. He felt exposed. Raw. Vulnerable. And he didn't like any of it.

He glanced at the grandfather clock. Chloe had been gone well over an hour. If she wasn't back in another fifteen minutes, he was going after her, no matter what his dragon thought of the idea. By then, Niall and the others would have materialized, and they could all go.

He wasn't at all certain he had enough power to win in a stand-off against his dragon, but between the four of them, something was bound to shake loose. He waited, fully expecting another lash from the dragon's tail to blister his back, but it didn't come.

"She is ours," the dragon said. *"'Tis why I took care to ensure another dragon bonded with her. We can fly together. Mate in the way we are meant to."*

A tableau painted in Technicolor precision unfurled as understanding zapped him. He rocked to a halt and rolled his shoulders back. "I'd have been delighted with any bond animal as her mate. One less dangerous than a dragon would have been fine. Hell, she could have remained a mage. I'd still care about her. If this plan of yours goes awry—" He shut up before he said words there was no backing down from.

"*It won't.*" The smug note was back.

Magic formed a glistening vortex, and Chloe shimmered into view. Relief steamrolled through him in great, blistering waves. He ran to her, catching her in his arms from behind. "Thank all the gods you're unharmed. I would have gone after you, but my dragon held me back." He stopped long enough to breathe. "It spoke true. The path you trod had no space for me."

He turned her in his arms, streamers of power still shimmering around her.

"You know, then?" She angled a blonde brow.

"Indeed, I do. And I welcome the first new dragon shifter in three hundred years." He kissed her forehead because she looked so appealing he needed to touch her. When she turned her face upward, the invitation obvious, he circumvented it. If he kissed her lush red lips, he'd be lost. He was so smitten by her, and she was so vulnerable from her first shift, they'd end up rutting on the carpet.

It wasn't how he wanted to take her, not their first time. An image of dragons mating midair blasted him, courtesy of his bondmate, and he blurted, "I can't wait to fly with you. We'll figure something out. Find a way where we don't reveal what we are."

She narrowed her eyes. "If you knew I was finding my bondmate, why were you worried about me?"

"Och, lassie." He switched to Gaelic to better manage his emotions; they ran hot and far too near the surface. "So much could have gone wrong. 'Tis a hard transition. You might not have lived through it, especially not at your age. Why do you think so few of us exist?"

Her expression twisted, and he helped himself to her thoughts as she relived the pain of her shift. His heart hurt for her, but he was pleased by how she'd risen to the occasion, not letting fear cripple her or weaken her resolve.

"Aye," he murmured, "the transition from skin to scales is a rocky one. Thanks be to all the gods, it gets easier."

"Same thing my dragon said." Pride lined her words when she said *my dragon*, and he smiled. She had every right to feel proud of herself.

Shifter magic shot through the room just before a portal formed admitting Sarai, Niall, and Stephan, all carrying books. Zee nodded to himself. They'd split up the burden, so they could teleport rather than drive. Made sense.

"Sorry it took so long." Stephan spoke Gaelic, following his apology with a word to close off his spell.

The portal transformed into a delicate mist before being absorbed by the ether.

"Aye. Fucking vampires thought to waylay us. Luckily, I had the foresight to bring a blade along." Despite his breezy assessment, Niall looked rattled. "Bollocks. I need a drink."

"Of course." Zee reluctantly let go of Chloe. She felt so good in his arms, it wasn't easy. He strode to a mirrored sideboard, pulled the doors open, and said, "Help yourself."

"After the vamps, it didn't seem prudent to burn up time driving," Stephan went on, "so we took as many books as we could teleport with. A few remain in Sarai's shop."

Zee turned around in time to see Sarai, brows furled, staring at Chloe. "Getting cozy, were you?" Her gaze developed an evaluative aspect. "Something is different."

Magic zinged from Sarai, weaving around Chloe, and Sarai's blue eyes widened. She shrieked. "I knew it," just before she dropped her books, threw herself on Chloe, and hugged her.

"Knew what, darling?" Niall asked from where he'd selected a bottle and was pouring himself a tumblerful of whiskey.

"If you weren't so rummy from killing vampires,

you'd have noticed." Sarai was still hugging Chloe. "She's a shifter now, just like us."

Niall whistled.

Stephan's harsh expression softened. He crossed the room and clapped Chloe on the back. "Congratulations, sister. Which animal selected you?"

Chloe extricated herself from Sarai's arms. Red splotched her cheekbones, but then everyone was staring at her. "My bondmate is a dragon. A beautiful red dragon with silver eyes."

Her eyes filled with tears. Zee started toward her, intent on comforting her, but brought himself up short. They were nothing to each other. They'd been fighting like squabbling family members before she'd been yanked into whatever spot the dragon had chosen.

"Holy godhead. A dragon?" Sarai's mouth fell open. "Oberon's balls, I'll have to run your chart again. Who was born first, you or Jeremiah?"

Chloe grinned through her tears. "You and your astrology. I was born first. Fifteen minutes earlier than my twin."

Sarai nodded sagely. "Fifteen minutes can make a lot of difference in astrology. I just assumed your data would be the same. Sloppy of me."

Niall placed a hand on her shoulder. "It will keep till later, darling. Right now, we have to get all those smart books in the same spot. Maybe they'll yield clues as to what to do next."

"Excellent redirect." Zachary offered Niall kudos for remaining on task. Usually, he was better at that, but he'd been so enticed, entranced, and excited about Chloe's transition, their whole reason for convening at his house had fled from center stage.

Stephan unhooked a pack he'd looped over one shoulder, and it fell to the floor. He knelt and extracted thick tomes with creased leather bindings. "Thought we'd begin with these," he said gruffly. "Or mayhap the ones Sarai brought."

After casting a sidelong glance at Chloe, still blinking away tears, Zachary murmured, "Of course." He started to make a run to the second-floor library when he had a better idea. "All my books are upstairs. Easier to move yours there than to bring mine down here. While you're doing that, I'll stop by the kitchen and bring the coffee pot and a few plates of goodies I put together."

Sarai bent and picked up the books she'd carried. "Where upstairs?" she asked.

"I suspect if we let magic lead us, it will take us to the correct spot," Stephan muttered and headed for the archway at the far end of the large room.

"It will," Zee concurred.

Chloe gathered her books; Niall snagged his, and

they followed the others as they filed out of the room and toward the main staircase.

Zee remained behind them until leaving the great room when he turned hard left for the kitchen. He thought about Chloe's description of the red dragon with silver eyes, and he was almost certain which dragon it had to be. He felt cowed at what an ass he'd made out of himself with his bondmate.

"I'm sorry," he told the dragon. "I was a dick."

"*You often are,*" the dragon agreed in a much too cheerful tone.

"You might have at least hesitated before agreeing with me." Zee walked into the kitchen and grabbed the coffee pot and a platter of biscuits, butter, and preserves. He'd always loved high tea and recreated it whenever the opportunity presented itself.

"*I might have,*" the dragon said, "*but I didn't.*"

"You'll have to tell me which other animals were agreeable to bonding with mages, but not right now."

The dragon didn't answer.

Zee only had two hands, so he used magic to coax another tray with sugar, cream, and cups to join him. Lastly, he lassoed an electric kettle with magical threads. Once he was certain he had everything, he cast a quick teleport spell and came out one floor up in front of a long, polished table where he set things down after rescuing them from where they hung suspended midair.

The others had sorted books along the table.

Chloe stood back and looked at the various volumes, thirteen of them total, and said to Zee, "Which ones of yours will you add to this mix?"

It was a decent question. He walked along rows of law books to a recessed panel that he touched lightly. It sprang inward, revealing a hidden room where he kept his magic books. He concealed them as insurance against theft, but they had a pesky habit of falling off shelves, moving about, and rustling pages when no one was touching them.

He had the occasional visitor—all human—in his law library, and such shenanigans would have been met with disbelief. Easier to not have to explain why a twenty-pound book just did a swan dive off a crowded shelf and was bouncing across the carpeted floor.

Niall whistled and followed him into the inner sanctum lined with ancient scrolls and dusty vellum. "Och and you're chock-full of tricks, mate."

Zee grinned, feeling better than he had in years. "Och back at you. All the better to engage in mysterious chicanery."

Niall snorted. "Why do I always feel like I need a dictionary around you?"

Sarai crowded inside, her eyes rounding into small

moons. "Oooh. Makes my collection look paltry." She dragged a book off a shelf.

Zee suppressed a desire to slap her hand. He had far too proprietary an interest in his books, and he had to get over seeing them as "his." They belonged to all shifters—mages too.

Oblivious to his inner turmoil, Sarai said, "This one. And perhaps these two." She pointed before adding them to the one already clasped in her arms.

"Hurry," Chloe called. "The pages are starting to turn on their own. Add the other books so the energy will be just right."

Sarai pushed past Zee and Niall and placed the books on the table. Zee exited the hidden room and let his gaze fall on each of the tomes. They were indeed in motion. Some spinning, some opening. "Did you already ask a question?"

Stephan shook his head. "Only in my mind, not out loud."

"It would have been enough," Zee said. "What did you ask?"

"What else?" Stephan twisted until his blue eyes burned into Zee. "I asked how we can eradicate vampires."

"Let's all ask the same question out loud," Sarai suggested.

Voices rose and fell around Zee, and then he kept

his eyes on the books. A few spun faster, like whirling dervishes, before opening of their own accord. Pages riffled and flipped. The air grew dusty and thick with the electric feel of expended power.

Chloe leaned over the first volume to quit moving, splaying her hands on either side of it. Her nostrils flared as she read, but she shook her head. "Let's wait and see what the other books have to say."

Zee resisted a temptation to join her, peer over her shoulder. He wanted to draw her against him, reassure her he'd protect her forever, but she wasn't the run-to-a-man type. Most modern women weren't, and the hard truth was he'd never figured out how to chip through their fierce independence.

He did okay tumbling the lassies into bed, but once he took charge of how their lives would play out, they ran like he'd doused them in hellsbane.

One by one, the remaining books came to a rest. He flicked the closest one around, so he could read it. Niall did the same, as did Stephan and Sarai. Zee clamped down on the epithet that jumped to the back of his throat, wanting out.

Niall saved him the trouble of hiding his disgust. "Bollocks." The jaguar shifter slapped his open hand down on the table. "We will find another way."

"Aye, that we will," Zee said.

"Hang on." Chloe's voice was strained. "Do the

books all say the same thing? We never compared them."

Zee cleared his throat and read, translating Egyptian as he went. "Mage magic empowers vampires. To vanquish the blood-sucking rogues, mages must be cordoned off, preferably on a borderworld. Absent mage magic, vampires will fade back into the darkness where they no longer pose a threat."

"Same thing mine says." Niall raked curved fingers through his dark hair. "But it makes no sense. Vampires are equal opportunity bastards. They can pull power from shifters as well as mages, and they've been clear we're their next target."

"Let's ask again," Stephan suggested. "I've rarely gotten a decent answer right off the blocks."

"Good idea," Sarai chimed in. She held out both hands. "Shall we join our power and include our bond animals?"

Zee grasped Sarai's hand on one side and Chloe's on the other. Her fingers were warm as they curled around his. "We will find a way that does not involve mass transport of mages away from Earth," he said.

"I never doubted it," she replied, tightlipped, "but thanks for your support."

It was far more than support. Gazing at her, taking

in the bleak determination streaming from her, he wanted to reassure her she'd never be alone again.

She might not want him, but he sure as hell wanted her.

"All together now," Stephan urged. "This time don't ask how to eradicate vamps, but how to ensure they can't use shifter or mage magic to power their workings."

Zee let the question roll from his lips. It was enough of a reframe, perhaps they'd get a different answer. The books went through the motions, even more rambunctious than they'd been before. If Zee hadn't known better, he'd have been certain they gloried in their freedom after sitting on shelves.

He watched the dancing vellum crinkle, fold, and unfold. Chloe's fingers tightened around his, and he squeezed back. When the rollicking books came to a rest at crazy angles from one another, he bent close, willing different words than he'd read before.

Not only were the words different, this time the language had shifted to Old English. His mouth split into a grim smile. "More like it," he said.

"Dangerous, but more my style." Stephan ran an index finger down the book he'd selected.

Zee inhaled briskly. No time to ask his bondmate's permission. Normally, things the animals shared were confidential. "My dragon says many bond animals stand ready to join with mages."

He stood straight, waiting for a blast of fire to build in his chest and explode out his mouth, but it never came.

"What are we waiting for?" Chloe quivered with excitement. "Let's get that ball rolling. The more shifters, the fewer of us who might fall into vampire clutches. They may have set their sights on shifters too, but mages are clearly easy pickings for them."

She tugged her hand from his, and their circle broke apart. No time for the coffee and tea he'd prepared. "We should return to your house," he told Chloe. "Let everyone know what we unearthed."

"Give me a moment." Sarai was typing madly into the display on her phone.

"What are you about?" Niall peered over his wife's shoulder.

"Charts. What else? Now I have Chloe's information, I can fine-tune hers and match it up with Zachary's."

"Stop right there." Chloe placed her hand across Sarai's screen. "It's good everyone's here. I have something to say."

"No need." Sarai batted Chloe's hand.

"Yeah. There is." She nodded toward Zee. "You've been kind to me, and I appreciate it, but there's so much more at stake here than synastry between your chart and mine. I have brand-new magic to learn about. We have a vampire horde to vanquish. I'm afraid if I lose sight of any of that—and if anyone could interrupt my concentration, it's you—I won't be the best warrior possible for our cause." She took on a wistful expression; it made her even more appealing.

"You're right." Sarai dropped her phone into her pocket. She glanced at the books. They'd quieted, but power zinged from one to the other. "I believe I'll leave mine here for the next day or so. They seem to complement one another, even with the few I left behind missing from the mix."

"I'll leave mine as well," Chloe said. "We may wish to return and consult with them."

For once, Zee was at a loss for words. He wanted to say so many things, convince Chloe they were stronger as a couple than apart, but he didn't give voice to any of them. Mostly because he understood words didn't exist that would bind her to his side.

She'd have to come to him in her own time. Or not at all. Magic shimmered as she worked up a travel spell.

"*Go with her,*" his dragon said. "*She's our mate.*"

"*Not if she doesn't wish it,*" he replied and readied power of his own.

There'd been a time when coming closer to

completing his library would have thrilled him, even if the other books were only on loan. Not anymore. He wanted Chloe, not books.

Getting to know himself, coming face to face with the insignificant things he'd hidden behind to mask an otherwise empty existence rankled, but he couldn't change the past.

As his spell took him, he wondered how the other mages would greet the news about their dragon-shifting kinswoman. With his mind wandering all over the place, he hoped to hell they'd accept the role the books had laid out for them.

Niall's assessment about danger had been a gross understatement, and most mages weren't exactly rabid warriors.

No point wasting energy in conjecture. They'll get with the program. Or not.

It was the *or not* part that posed a problem. Anyone who didn't sign on risked death by mage fire. Chloe had assumed all her kin would jump at the chance to fight in the vampire war. Zee wasn't so certain.

If he was right, it would break her heart.

CHAPTER 6

*C*hloe's travel spell snatched her up faster than she'd anticipated. It would take time to get used to how the dragon augmented her power. A bad case of nerves soured her stomach. Not about her new bondmate, though. That part of things felt settled, right. The other mages would be thrilled for her. Jeremiah had been the sacrificial sheep in that regard. Having accepted him, they'd accept her.

Her worries were how her kinfolks would react to forced conscription in the vampire war. Those living with her would pick up the banner, some with more enthusiasm than others. Although she'd put up a brave front, she wasn't at all sure about those outside her immediate circle. No one reacted well when choice was stripped from them, and some mages would be angry and resentful. Mulish enough to outright refuse.

Vampires hadn't bothered them, so why should they inconvenience themselves? She winced. She'd run up against that attitude during their long-running war with shifters back in the Old Country. Unlike shifters, mages were far from natural warriors. They didn't jump up and embrace danger.

As she weighed the two messages the books had shown, they weren't all that different. The first had taken the tack that mages fueled vampire treachery, so the wisest course was to move them far enough away vamps couldn't strip mine their power. The second allowed mages to remain so long as they fought on the front lines right along with their shifter cousins. It was clear, though, that refusing to fight would be a death sentence.

The edict was harsh, but it made sense. It was far too risky allowing mages to sit this one out. Vampires could find them and do exactly what they'd done with the other mages they'd turned into minions. What the books hadn't laid out, but was implicit, was any mage choosing to ally himself with vampires would be killed in the most expeditious way possible.

No more nicey-nicey separating mages from their magic instead of killing them.

The sick feeling she'd started with intensified. It was one thing to lose strangers, but what if some of the perfidious mages were ones she knew?

"Doesn't matter. Treachery is treachery," rang through her head.

Breath whooshed from her, and she almost lost control of her travel spell. She hadn't forgotten about her new bondmate. How could she? But nor was she expecting it to pop up with opinions.

"Ha. Get used to it." A deep, rumbly chuckle vibrated in her breastbone. *"Back to the other. Don't waste your sympathy on those who don't deserve it."*

The black of her travelling spell was ceding to gray, which meant she was almost at her destination. She'd have smiled if the situation weren't so grim. So far, having a bondmate added a combination of mother and conscience to the mix.

"Not sympathy, so much," she replied. *"More..."* Her thoughts floundered. More, what? Since when did knowing someone for hundreds of years make them worthier of salvage than a brand-new acquaintance?

"Better," the dragon murmured.

"You read my thoughts, huh?"

"Indeed. All of them."

At least it didn't tack "get used to it" on the end.

The dragon wasn't done, though. It continued, *"Wars mean loss. No way around it. Keep your eye on who's left standing at the end. It's what's important. Not so much how we got there, but that we got there at all. That someone on our side is, indeed, still on their feet to celebrate a victory.*"

She'd never been an end-justifies-the-means person, but she didn't want to argue she'd have to live with herself—and what she'd done—if she was one of those left when the dust settled.

The walls of her bedroom shimmered around her, coming into focus, and she loosed her spell. She'd wanted a moment to gather herself and her thoughts before facing everyone. It was why she'd chosen her room rather than any of the downstairs locations. She had to tell everyone about her transformation, but she didn't want to just blurt it out. Such momentous news also didn't lend itself to a casual, oh-by-the-way statement.

"*If there's a bigger space than this one, why not show them?*" the dragon suggested slyly.

"Might be a bit overwhelming." Chloe aimed for diplomacy. The reality of eight feet of winged dragon would be far more than overwhelming. Terrifying was more like it. Even though mages were magical creatures, the sheer bulk of the dragon, along with its whirling silver eyes, would take some getting used to.

"*Perhaps you're right.*" The dragon adopted a thoughtful tone. "*We can begin by telling them. What are we waiting for? Zachary and the others are below. I sense them.*"

Chloe trotted to her closet and pulled out a fresh shirt and pair of slacks. "Give me a moment. I want to change."

"Why? You're not dirty."

Lying to her bondmate was out of the question. So was not answering at all. "I'm questing about for the best way to announce our, erm, association."

"You underestimate those who live here." The dragon's tone was dry.

As if its words held power of their own, a staunch knock was followed by her door flying open. Jeremiah raced to her and wrapped his arms around her. "I'm still pissed about Mitch and the lore books, but I am happy for you, sister. You've wanted this for a long time."

The corners of her mouth twitched. If Jer knew, so did everyone else. She sent warm thoughts inward to her dragon. *"Looks as if you were right."*

"I always am," it retorted.

She wriggled free from her brother's embrace and rolled her eyes. "Thanks. Of the two of us, I was who wanted a bond animal." She laid her crushed clothing aside, draping it over a chair to encourage the wrinkles to hang out.

"True enough. While I did my damnedest to be a good soldier and play the hand I'd been dealt." He grinned crookedly, his joy for her genuine and palpable.

Renee dashed into the room, her blonde hair wet from a recent shower. She shoved Jeremiah out of the way and hugged Chloe. "Welcome to the pack, sister-in-law." Letting go, she stepped far enough back to examine Chloe with interest. "A dragon, eh? Maybe if we draped enough magic around the backyard, you could shift for us. It's been many a long year since I've laid eyes on one of the mythical creatures."

Heat built in Chloe's belly until smoke erupted from her mouth. When she was done coughing, she gasped, "The dragon doesn't like to be called mythical. They're real."

Renee bowed her head. When she straightened, she said, "Sorry, oh ancient one. Poor choice of words on my part. I love and revere what you are as does my eagle."

The torrent of smoke had ceded to steam. Even that ceased, and Chloe sucked air deep into her lungs. She looked from her brother to his mate and felt heat rise to her face. "I was in here trying to find the best way to tell everybody," she admitted.

"They already know." Jeremiah's face took on a stern expression. "Give your housemates a smattering of credit."

The heat intensified, but she met her twin's direct

gaze. "Do they know the rest? What the books said we have to do?"

Renee shook her head, sending droplets of water flying every which way. "Nope. Zee said we had to wait for you."

Chloe nodded briskly. "Let's get to it, then. First hurdle seems to be behind me." She didn't add the next one was much higher.

Ever a gentleman, Jeremiah stood aside and motioned both her and his mate ahead of him. She trotted down the familiar risers, taking them two at a time. When she hurried into the great room, everyone looked at her.

"There you are." Zee caught her gaze and smiled ruefully. "My bondmate was giving me hell about going up to roust you out."

"Here I am," she agreed and swallowed around a dry place in her throat. "Maybe you should take the lead on this?"

He shook his head. "These are your people. They'll respect what you have to say, offer it credence they might not afford what comes out of my mouth."

"Oh for the love of Arianrhod, just get on with it." Raul pinned her with his hazel gaze.

Chloe balanced on the balls of her feet, unsure quite where to begin. An adage advising Keep it Simple, Stupid, rattled through her head. At first, she thought it came courtesy of her dragon, but the creature remained silent. She felt it within her, though, watchful and wary.

She rolled her shoulders as straight as she could make them. "We, uh that is Niall, Sarai, Stephan, Zachary, and I, consulted our combined books."

"*Coward,*" the dragon muttered.

Steam wafted from her mouth, and she grimaced. "My bondmate just censured me for walking around the point. I'll cut to the meat of things. We asked the books two questions and chose to go with their second answer."

"Well?" Johnny waggled two fingers her way. "Out with it, Missy."

She inhaled briskly. "Every mage must join the fight against vampires. Bond animals wait to link with some of you, but even those who remain unbonded must fight. No one sits this one out." She let her gaze track around the room, and added, "No one," for emphasis.

Breath rattled from her throat as she waited for a response.

"All right," Raul said in measured tones. "So we're all being conscripted. Correct?" At her nod, he went on. "What happens if one of us refuses the call?"

She steeled herself to hold his gaze. "They must die. We cannot risk any more mages being turned into magical fodder by vampires." Chloe hurried on. "Not much we can do about those who sign on willingly. They've underwritten their own death warrants by their treachery. But the same fate—death by magefire—awaits innocent bystanders, those who hate conflict and would prefer not to fight."

A collective intake of breath rattled around the room from mage to mage. A few looked shocked. "You'd turn on your own simply because they opt for nonviolent solutions?" Raul's wife, Stella, spoke up. She raked red hair streaked with blonde away from her face.

Raul twined a protective arm around her but didn't say anything.

Jeremiah followed her question with one of his own. "Do you see any other way?"

Stella's forehead creased into a thoughtful mass of wrinkles. "When you ask it that way," she spoke slowly, "perhaps not. So long as we sit on the sidelines, vampires could tap our magic, like they did to those poor unfortunates you found shackled in that cave."

"Exactly." Jeremiah's tone was cold.

Chloe knew what that day had cost him when he'd called magefire to kill over fifty of their kin. He stood straight, a resolute expression cutting deep into his normally pleasant expression.

"What about all the other mages?" Johnny asked. "The ones not in this room."

"We have to contact the closest ones and work outward from there," Chloe said. "In turn, those we speak with must pass the message on. Eventually, it will reach us all."

"I fear eventually may take too long," Zachary's deep voice boomed from the rear of the large room.

Chloe turned to him and crossed her arms beneath her breasts. "If you have a better idea, let's hear it."

"How many mage groups are there in North America?"

"I'm not sure," Jeremiah cut in. "Are you thinking this problem is unique to us?"

Zee hesitated before answering. "I have no way of knowing for certain, but I will see what knowledge I can gather from other dragon shifters. Unless vampires have staged a stealthy comeback worldwide, my first guess is the problem is localized to North America."

Chloe thought about it. "If that's correct, the simplest solution might be moving."

"Wouldn't work," Stephan growled. "They'd follow us. Vampires are as mobile as we are. They teleport, and they've had a taste of what mage power can do for them. Not that they'll be stopping there. The day they captured Renee, they made it quite clear they plan to spread their poison through shifter ranks too."

Niall strode to the center of the room. "A point I've tried to make—one that doesn't seem to have sunk in—is there is no more us and them. We are one magical race encompassing shifters and mages. We must reclaim our mutual heritage."

Chloe inhaled briskly. "Assuming you're correct, and I believe you are, we need to make certain all the shifters are on board, right along with the mages."

"Shifters already are." Stephan rolled his shoulders back. "Our network is efficient because of the animals."

"Circling back to strategy," Zachary said, "word of mouth isn't fast enough. Leverage telepathy and any other means mages have developed to broadcast critical information. If we're very lucky, the vampire problem hasn't spread outside this continent. No reason why it should have. This seems to be the breeding ground for their initial experimentation leveraging added power."

"So if we move fast and strike hard"—Chloe clenched her jaw—"we can halt the spread here."

"My opinion," Zachary agreed. "And I hope to hell my assumptions are correct."

The hum of conversation rose and fell. She tuned into bits and pieces of it, waiting as everyone got used to the idea of becoming a foot soldier. Zachary crossed the room, heading right toward her. Part of her was pleased, but another wanted to turn aside. No way to avoid him without being obvious about it, though, so she waited until he was close before asking, "What happens next?"

"Funny thing, but it's why I sought you out." He drew his ruddy brows together. "What a pity vampires don't live in seethes anymore."

"It would make things easier," she agreed. "Finding them all in one spot and weak as the dickens during daylight."

"They require mage magic to operate during the day, right?"

Chloe nodded. "It appears so. And the fact they waylaid Niall and his group when they were getting the lore books suggests they didn't have to hunt too long or too hard for more mages to mesmerize."

"Makes sense. Once they got the feel of you, your scent, they're exceptional trackers." He hesitated a beat. "I wanted to float something by you."

Something about his tone caught her attention. He sounded uncertain, which hadn't been her experience of him thus far. "Is anything wrong?"

"*Not wrong. Not exactly.*" He switched to telepathy, apparently not interested in being overheard. "*I'm normally steady, unflappable. It's what makes the law such a perfect profession for me. I can preside over grisly cases and leave them in the courtroom when I go home."*

She angled a sidelong glance his way. Why was he confiding in her? They barely knew one another. He was hot and hunky and got her juices flowing, but none of that mattered. When he didn't offer anything further, she prodded, "So you're usually levelheaded. Did something change?"

"Telepathy please." The same sense of unease she'd picked up before grew stronger.

"Sure. Of course." She waited, wondering what could have impacted his equanimity.

Hooking an arm beneath hers, he drew her to an unoccupied corner of the room. Jeremiah and Niall and Stephan had begun sketching something on a whiteboard propped on an easel, but she focused all her attention on Zee.

"I may have mentioned there aren't many dragon shifters. Until you, I was the only one in North America."

"Where are the others?"

"They used to be in the northern reaches of Asia. We tend to like colder climes." He swallowed before continuing. *"Long ago, the others told me I should join them, but I ignored the invitation. I got a lot of grief for my decision from them—and my bondmate."*

Anxiety dug its claws in deep. *"Are you considering*

leaving?" He was strong magically. They could use his help to obliterate the vampires, but that was her agenda. In truth, he owed them nothing. Words swarmed in the back of her throat, but she refused to utter any of them. Things like her needing him to teach her and the group needing his magic were obvious.

Either he remained because he wanted to—not because he'd been guilt-tripped—or his resentment would taint both his magic and theirs.

A shocked look rippled over his high forehead, square chin, and stubble-covered cheeks. *"Yes, but not in the way you meant it."*

"How would you know what I meant?" She slapped a ward around her mind, not interested in him plumbing her thoughts.

His nostrils flared, and he tightened his fingers around her arm. They were warm and enticing. His scent—heather, gorse, and lilac—bloomed around her. It was tough not to lean into him, inhaling eagerly.

"We could use help," he said. *"I'm not terribly hopeful my dragon-shifting kinfolks will even hear me out—they were furious at my refusal to join them—but perhaps our need is great enough to convince them to grant us an audience."*

"You said us. Why? Plus, if there's a point, I missed it." She was so flummoxed, she dropped back to spoken speech.

"Damn, but I'm making a total botch of this. Me, the one who bends words to his will for a living. Sorry. It will take time for the others in this room to get the word out to every mage group. While they're about it, we could travel to where I believe my kinsmen reside. They will want to meet you, and perhaps a new dragon shifter will soften their hearts toward me, make them more amenable to listening and offering aid."

She yanked out of his grasp. "You want to use me as some kind of conciliatory offering?" Her voice had shrilled, but she didn't care who heard her.

He leveled his dark-blue gaze at her and gave up on telepathy. "What is it about you that you choose the worst possible interpretation?"

Fury blazed a path through her. "Not only do you want to use me, now you're casting disparaging interpretations of my motives? Who the fuck do you think you are?"

Magic blazed around her, so potent it singed her skin. When it cleared, they were in the fenced-in backyard. She stood tall. "I did not give you permission to move me."

The corners of his mouth twitched. "Nay, you did not, but I'm not keen on holding private conversations in front of others. What we have to say is between us. I am going to teleport to northern Asia in the vicinity of

Siberia. I believe it would be in everyone's best interest for you to join me."

"We should go," her dragon spoke up.

Chloe ground her teeth. *"Why?"* she asked her bondmate. *"He's exploiting us."*

Zee just watched her, obviously listening in.

"He's trying to help you. You should meet the other dragon shifters. Someday, you may have need of them. He knows where they are."

"I bet you do too," she countered.

"Neither here nor there. I like his plan. The addition of dragon magic may make all the difference persuading vampires to retreat to their disgusting shadows."

When she glanced at Zee, he'd quirked a brow her way. "I hadn't expected support from your bondmate, but I'm most humbly grateful for its vote of confidence."

She pressed her lips together and pushed her reservations aside—for the moment. "Shifter magic is new to me. I could use assistance learning how to manage it. I propose a trade."

His twitching lips gave up and formed a grin. "Done."

"But you haven't heard my proposition," she protested. "I might ask you to fly to the moon and bring me back moon rocks."

He shook his head. "Nay. You want me to mentor

you. In exchange, you'll accompany me to Asia. It's a more than fair trade, one that's already begun on my side of things."

Chloe thought back to their conversation after her first shift and realized he spoke true. She smothered the smile that wanted out. "I always was a lousy bargainer. Maybe I should steepen my request."

"Up to you, sweetheart." He held up both hands. "No disrespect meant."

"None taken." She didn't tell him hearing the world sweetheart roll off his tongue had given her a little thrill that began at the base of her spine and zipped over the top of her head.

He held out a hand. "Deal?"

She clasped it, loving the feel of his fingers as they closed around hers. "Deal."

They stood like that, hands joined, for a few beats too long. Deep within her, the dragon hummed, and the unrelated notes made it harder to let go of Zee's hand.

"We should go inside and tell the others," he said at last.

"We should." She extricated her fingers from the heat of him but couldn't manage to rip her gaze away from his restless-ocean eyes. Chloe gave herself a brisk mental slap. If there was ever a time not to go all gaga over a man, this was it.

"How long will we be gone?" she asked, keeping her tone formal. "And will I need to bring anything?"

"Not more than a day. We'll teleport, so you won't need anything beyond the clothes on your back."

"But won't such a long trip drain your magic?"

"Nay, lassie. Shouldn't be a problem. Besides, your power will be included in the mix."

The farthest she'd gone on her own was five states over, and she'd had to rest up for a few hours before returning. "What will I need?"

"Warm clothes, but unless something has changed we'll spend most of our time there as dragons."

She grinned, liking the idea. Her first flight had been far too short, and she wanted more.

He matched her smile. "Excellent, and yes I helped myself to your thoughts. Gather what you need. I'll let the others know what we're about and make certain they have a solid plan on board to reach all of your kin."

"Sounds good. I'll be downstairs in a few minutes."

No easy way to leave him, so she turned and loped up the back steps. She admired his ability to take charge and look for ways to make all of them stronger, but part of her chafed at giving up even an angstrom of control. He'd crafted a plan. First, she'd balked, but then she'd agreed.

Was she growing soft? Would she turn into one of

those clinging females who waited for a man to tell them what to do?

"Get over yourself," the dragon hissed. *"We need to do this. You're not who you used to be, and the new you has yet to emerge. Trust you'll like her just as well as you liked yourself when you were a mage."*

It was good advice, and she ran with it as she donned a warm jacket, hat, and gloves. She already wore thick boots. In less than five minutes, she was walking down the stairs to meet Zee. Times might be harsh, but adventure beckoned. Excitement thrummed through her at the prospect. What lay before her would make her stronger.

And she'd be lying if she didn't admit she craved time with Zachary. He had a vulnerable side, one he'd revealed earlier. Surely it meant he trusted her...

Nah. He needs me and was willing to do whatever it took to make me capitulate.

Irritation at playing into his hand resurfaced, but she pushed it aside. Her bondmate was correct. None of this was about her. They had a mission, one she had to keep in clear view. Nothing else mattered. If she had to abase herself eleven ways from Sunday to gain the other dragons' cooperation in the vampire war, she would.

Christ! I'm exactly the same as Zee, willing to do anything so long as it achieves what I want.

The thought centered and repelled her as she pelted downstairs. Zachary waited at the bottom. "I talked with your brother and Niall. Everything is in play on their end. Ready to go?"

She nodded and felt power build around them. When it cleared, she'd ask for details about what the others would be doing while they were gone. For now, she leaned into the characteristic feel of Zee's magic. It surrounded her, soothing and inflaming by turns. She could lose herself in the feel of his power.

"Open your magic to me, lass," he instructed.

"Sorry," she mumbled, having forgotten she needed to help.

"No apologies needed." His eyes gleamed warmly and took on a whirling aspect just like her dragon's.

"What color are you?" she blurted, and then clapped a hand over her mouth. "Never mind."

"Dark midnight blue. I wondered when you'd get around to asking." He grabbed both her hands. "Hang on tight, and we'll be gone from here."

She stopped fighting her attraction and gripped his hands. His magic bubbled, hot and viscous; the walls of her home fell away, yielding to darkness.

CHAPTER 7

Zee kept a firm hold on Chloe, both physically and with strands of his magic woven in with her own, as he kindled his transport spell. He'd been a blundering idiot when he'd dragged her into the yard. Driven by need, hot, fierce, primal, he'd acted before he thought. He was damned fortunate she hadn't slapped him and vanished back inside. Yet for some unknown reason, she'd heard him out, despite her outrage at his unforgiveable, Neanderthal behavior.

He struggled for words to thank her but couldn't come up with any that didn't sound lame. Besides, in the spirit of absolute honesty, given the same situation, he'd do the same thing all over again.

What did that make him?

A total dick, he answered himself. His dragon had

cheerfully agreed with that assessment, and it knew him better than anyone.

"Do you have a plan for after we get there?" Chloe asked, her voice soft in his mind.

Her question dragged him out of his critical mindset. He could do all the negative introspection he wanted to—but later. *"Not exactly,"* he admitted.

"So we'll be winging it?"

He tightened his grip on her hands, loving the touch of her skin against his fingers. *"The trick will be getting them to talk with us."*

"I don't understand."

"They have every reason to turn their scaled hides on me. I walked away from their fellowship. Dragon shifters fancy themselves at the top of the shifter hierarchy. It wasn't always like that. We only developed notions of grandeur after migrating to the States."

"Why would it happen then and not before?"

It was a good question. *"Not sure, exactly. Maybe once we had a larger space to spread out, the necessity of getting along faded. Some of us never felt we had much in common with, for example, coyote or bird shifters."*

"Mmph. Maybe it's not such a bad thing dragons put a lot of distance between themselves and other shifters," she offered in thoughtful tones.

"What do you mean?"

"I suspect other shifters, those who aren't dragons,

don't view themselves as inferior, and they'd launch one campaign after the next to disabuse dragons of the notion they're special."

Zee offered her points for sharp insight. *"You just nailed the precise reason they left. One too many internecine spats."* He paused a beat before going on. *"On the one hand, they're probably still angry with me. On the other, they'll be pleased we recognize their magic as powerful and are soliciting aid."*

"I see. It will be a matter of moving them from how they feel about you to focusing on being needed."

"Exactly." He sent out a few test strands to assess the progress of his travel spell. *"We'll be there soon, and regardless of how they feel about me, they will be thrilled and delighted about you."*

"Surely, they've added to their ranks."

"I'm fairly sure they haven't. It would require a dragon from the animals' world offering a bond. They're even more insular than the shifters they bond with, so it's not a frequent event."

"But if two dragon shifters mate, isn't the result...?" Her words trailed off.

"Not necessarily. Shifters mating does produce other shifters, but not necessarily of the same variety. We dream our bondmates beginning when we're children. The bond establishes itself somewhat later, but well before adulthood."

"*I can see where two dragons producing, say, a wolf, might be a problem,*" she muttered. "*Parents are supposed to support their children, make them believe they're gifted, special. It's rather difficult to do if you're convinced your kid is inferior because their bondmate is an owl or a coyote.*"

"*You just identified the second reason dragon shifters removed themselves from shifter society. Dragon shifter children weren't dreaming any animals, probably because none of the animals wished to place themselves in an untenable situation. Bond animals are intensely loyal—to their bondmate. If it was pressed or ridiculed, a non-dragon child's bondmate might fuel the discontent by forcing shifts to prove its worth.*"

"*Hmmm. I can see where that wouldn't go well.*"

He wasn't quite sure how the next words happened, but he blurted, "*I really like you. You have a wonderfully incisive mind,*" before he could stop himself.

"*Incisive mind, eh?*" Amusement laced into her words. "*Coming from you, that's high praise, indeed.*"

He chuckled. "*Thanks. I take myself far too seriously.*"

"*Ya think?*"

Before he could come up with a snappy reply, she went on, "*You don't exactly have a corner on that market. I'm an architect, but I walked away from a successful firm I built from the ground up."*

"Why?"

"I loved the creative part, crafting something holding to the ragged edges of what each material was capable of. After a decade, though, most of my time was spent dealing with irate customers, nasty building inspectors, corporate gurus telling me my design was 'lovely, but wouldn't stand up to a stiff wind.'"

He waited, wanting to know everything about the woman linked to him by magic and his travel spell.

"Jer knew how miserable I was, how the light had gone out of my life. One day, he sat me down and asked what was in it for me. Made me stop spinning my wheels long enough to realize I didn't need the money— or the aggravation. I also didn't need Fuller & Associates to draft building plans. I could do it on my own if I wanted."

"So you walked away?" His opinion of her, already high, shot through the ceiling.

"More or less. I sold the firm to a group of three of my junior partners five years ago and never looked back."

"I want to hear more about things you've designed, but we'll be at our destination very soon."

True to his words, black was already shading to gray and the pull of gravity returning. He summoned power to cushion their transition as they rolled onto a desolate stretch of rocky beach. Ice stretched outward in slabs and chunks, and the bleak cries of seabirds wheeling overhead filled his ears. The salt-tang of the sea filled his nostrils, and he inhaled deeply. He'd missed the ocean with its restless tides. Not much saltwater in Colorado.

Chloe tugged her hands from his and tucked them beneath her arms. A brisk wind ruffled her hair around her and threatened to snatch the woolen cap from her head. He wished he'd borrowed a hat and gloves from Jeremiah or one of the other mages, but he could live with being cold.

She shielded her eyes with a hand, scanning the skies. "Where are the other dragons?"

"We'll find them. But it's far more likely they'll find us."

Chloe focused on him. "How can you know?"

"Because I catch bits and pieces of their magic. Come on." He moved toward a stark, gray band of cliffs about fifty feet from the shoreline. Dotted with caves, it was a perfect spot to leave their clothes where the wind wouldn't pick them up and blow them out to sea.

He ducked through an opening, relieved to be out of the incessant wind.

"What are we doing?" she asked.

When he looked at her, ice clung to her eyelashes,

lending her a fairytale appearance. "We needed a spot to leave our clothing. We'll strip and call shift magic, and then we'll hustle outside so we have room for our bodies to grow."

Color dotted her cheeks that had been white from cold.

Zee softened his tone. "You're lovely, Chloe, but this isn't an awkward seduction attempt. We'll need our clothes later to teleport back to Colorado. This is a decent spot to leave them. If you shift with them on—"

She waved him to silence and offered a rueful smile. "I know. Last time, my dragon told me to undress. This time, it's you. Maybe next time, I'll figure it out on my own."

He moved farther into the cave and started by removing his boots. Maybe if he set an example, it would make it easier for her to leave her garments behind. Shifters didn't have much in the way of body modesty. When you grew up moving from form to form, it often left you naked, sometimes with your clothes in tatters if you didn't plan well. Chloe would get with the program, but it might take some time.

He was down to shirt and trousers, taking care to face the wall and offer her at least an illusion of privacy, when she said. "Okay. I'm ready. And my dragon is champing at the bit."

Zee skinned out of his remaining clothes, adding

them to the pile in front of him and dropping a decent-sized rock over everything for good measure. He turned slowly, trying not to ogle her, and failing utterly. Blonde hair fell to waist level, but two pert nipples peeked through the curtain of hair. Shapely muscles ran across her shoulders and down her upper arms. Hips flared from a slender waist, and a mat of golden curls nested in the vee between her legs. Long, well-formed legs that made him long for them wrapped around him.

That last thought was his undoing, and his cock began to thicken where it hung between his legs. Anxious to escape her scrutiny, which was nearly as intense as his, he left their shelter at a lope, calling shift magic as he went.

"I tell you, she is ours. Ours," his dragon trumpeted into his mind.

Zee ignored both his bondmate and the sexual heat roaring through him. He welcomed the stretching sensation as bones rearranged themselves and skin ceded to scales. Once he was more dragon than man, he risked a look at Chloe. Wings were just forming, and a gout of flame shot from her mouth.

By all the goddesses who ever walked, she was even more gorgeous as a dragon than she'd been as a human. Zee, who'd always held himself aloof from entanglements, fell and fell hard. Maybe it was the extra push from his bondmate, but he was smitten.

A harsh cry blasted from him—a dragon mating cry. He clenched his jaws firmly shut to avoid another escaping. Maybe she wouldn't recognize it.

"Nice try." His dragon savored its freedom, and its ascendency. *"Even if she doesn't, her bondmate will."*

Wings spread, Chloe's red dragon ran down the beach. Zee sent a wave of magic to lift her from the earth, make her transition to flight easier. He'd spent his first century hunting for cliffs to jump from. While crags sat behind them, he didn't want to waste time climbing to the top of them.

The red dragon trumpeted.

He trumpeted back and leapt into the air, wings beating hard as he gained altitude. The joy he'd always derived from flying filled him to bursting. To have another dragon to share the ecstasy made it ten times better. He hadn't shared the skies with anything but birds for far too long.

Even though they had serious business to attend to, he couldn't resist banking and diving right along with Chloe. Her delight was contagious, and he imagined what it must be like to discover flight after decades shackled to earth.

Zee caught himself up short. That attitude, the one where dragons had a better deal than anyone else, had been the death knell for them coexisting with other shifters. They had to move past it.

Chloe flew a figure eight and came out of it puffing fire. Her silver eyes glowed with happiness, and the desire that had speared him at the sight of her naked body returned with a vengeance. Dragon lust was harsher than human, far more immediate. As his cock swelled, curved against the small scales lining his belly, he blew steam, followed by the same mating bugle as before. It slipped out despite his best efforts to contain it.

Chloe's dragon twisted midair, eyes whirling faster as it regarded him. His dragon was more than ready for the aerial mating dance unique to dragons, but Chloe's was thinking about it, not ready to commit.

Because it would be a commitment. Once mated in dragon form, their lives would be sealed together forever by the mate bond. He searched for words to tell her—in case her dragon didn't, but a staunch blast of magic hit him full in the chest.

He jerked his head upward, scanning the skies. Sure enough, half a dozen dragons winged toward them. Red. Gold. Black. Green. Blue. They flew with an easy grace that made him proud of what he was.

"*Follow us,*" blasted through his head, and the winged contingent wheeled as a unit, heading inland.

Zachary waited for Chloe to fly after the other

dragons, but she held back. *"It's all right."* He switched to shielded telepathy. It wouldn't do for the other dragons to mock Chloe for her reticence.

She glided after the flight, and he fell in next to her, keeping pace with her wingbeats. He wanted to reassure her it was a positive sign the dragons had located them so quickly, but it might be a very bad omen as well.

Surely, they hadn't spent the last two centuries lying in wait for him to show up. Dragons had long memories and were notorious grudge holders, but to still be pissed at him bordered on the absurd.

Half an hour later, they were still flying. Chloe was tiring; he felt it in the droop of her wings before she lifted them. He created an air cushion with magic and positioned it beneath her.

"Thanks. I was fading," she said in a strained voice. *"Do you know where we're going?"*

"I think so." Zee angled a wingtip. *"See that mountain range? There used to be a cave system within it large enough to accommodate us in wyrm form."*

Sure enough, the lead dragon, a gold named Eran, altered course, heading right for where Zee remembered. He maintained the padding beneath Chloe until she touched down. It offered her a more elegant landing. By the time he joined her, the other dragons had marched inside.

He draped a wing across her back and nudged gently. Together, they walked beneath an arched opening inscribed with runic markings. The entry cave was as he remembered it. An urn sat dead center with a flame burning. Powered by magic, it never went out. Stalagmites and stalactites dotted the space, some so large they joined one another. The limestone formations glowed a pale, luminous green in light from the fire.

The next archway brought them into a far larger cave. Perhaps two hundred feet round and lit by sconces lining the earthen walls. Dragons lounged within the circle. A quick head count yielded fifty-two, but there could easily be more out of sight within the extensive cavern system. At the point Zachary defected, there'd been something like eighty-four dragon shifters in this group.

Eran lumbered close. *"You have returned to us."*

"Aye and nay."

Smoke puffed from Eran's open jaws, and he angled his gaze at Chloe. *"A new dragon shifter. What magic is this? We have not added to our ranks since you left."*

Chloe's scales clanked as she stood tall. *"I am right here. Do not discuss me as if I were an object."* She was panting.

Zee figured she was exhausted from flying so far

her second time airborne. He rebuked himself for indulging in the aerial ballet right after they arrived.

Retreating to custom, Zee bowed slightly. "*Open skies and air beneath your wings, Eran.*"

"*Open skies to you as well,*" their flight leader responded automatically.

"*I bring less than good news, I fear,*" Zee went on. "*Might we shift and talk more easily?*" He waited, fully expecting Eran to tell him he could deliver whatever he'd come to say in dragon form or not at all. Zee wanted to give Chloe a break from using magic to do anything. Even telepathy required power, and hers needed a spot of recovery time.

Eran narrowed his whirling golden eyes until only their green centers remained visible. "*Aye, I can accommodate your request. Robes are in the same spot within.*"

"*Where shall we meet you?*" Zee asked.

"*Inner council chamber.*"

"*We'll be there in less than five minutes.*" Zee lumbered across the room, grateful Chloe followed without balking. He led her down a twisting corridor and into a side chamber lined with large wooden armoires.

Once there, he summoned shift magic, yanking open wardrobe doors as soon as talons turned to fingers. He'd just withdrawn two fur-lined garments crafted of heavy wool when he heard a long, drawn-out moan from Chloe.

He turned, robes in hand, to see her hunched on the packed earthen floor, shivering. "Goddammit, Chloe. You used too much magic."

"Tell me something I don't know," she muttered through chattering teeth.

He hustled to where she knelt, drew her to her feet, and wrapped the heavier of the robes around her. Next he drew her into his arms, letting the warmth of his body penetrate the garment around her. She felt incredible pressed against him, but he'd be worse than a cad to take advantage of her weakness. When she stopped shivering, he draped the other robe around himself.

"Come on," he urged. "We'll get you something restorative to drink."

Her gaze skittered away from his. "Sorry. I'll do a better job pacing myself. My dragon warned me, but I thought I knew more than it did." She rolled her eyes. "Stupid of me."

"I thought you said five minutes." Eran strode into the room in human form. Golden hair woven with gemstones, no doubt part of his hoard, trailed to his feet, and his green eyes snapped with annoyance.

Chloe bowed low, swaying a bit before straightening. "Do not blame him. I'm the problem. I'm very new at this. Today was only my second flight, and I'm afraid I overdid things. My dragon warned me, but..."

Eran squared his broad shoulders until he took full advantage of his six-foot-four-inch height. "I would hear this tale. To join our ranks from adulthood is unheard of."

Chloe staggered; Zachary wrapped an arm around her. "Lead out. Once we find chairs, I'll get Chloe something to drink."

"Is she your mate?" Eran's bald question shocked Zee.

"I'm no one's mate," Chloe spoke for herself.

"Excellent." Eran's normally dour expression lightened. "We have many unattached men who would like naught better than a lissome wench such as you."

Fire spewed from Zee's mouth. Before he could follow the flames with some scathing comment like they'd have to fight their way past his claim—never mind she didn't know about it—Chloe saved him the trouble. She offered Eran a small, tight smile. "We've not been formally introduced." She held out her hand. "My name is Chloe Fuller."

"I am Eran Goldsson, and it's a pleasure to meet you, Chloe." He released her hand.

"The pleasure is mutual. Before you go spreading the word I'm up for grabs"—she sent a pointed look

Eran's way—"I'm not. Zachary and I come on serious business that far transcends anything as trivial as—"

Eran made a chopping motion. "I get the picture, young dragon. Afore you leave, we shall ensure you understand establishing a mate bond with one of your kin is your paramount duty."

"Oh, really?" Chloe hooked a thumb toward Zee. "He didn't."

"He's male. Being unattached is allowed, but not precisely sanctioned." Eran's tone had cooled considerably, but Zachary was delighted Chloe was standing up to him.

"Can the lecture on dragon customs wait?" he inquired, keeping his tone carefully neutral.

Eran curled his lip into a sneer. "I had hopes you'd finally come to your senses, Zachary Marston. I fear I was mistaken."

"The inner council chamber?" Zee pressed, sidestepping Eran's rebuke.

Eran spun on his heel in a plume of smoke. Zee repressed an inane desire to laugh. He'd wanted to tell the old bastard off for years, and this was as close as he'd ever come.

Chloe elbowed him. "When were you going to get around to telling me dragon shifters were a bunch of paternalistic assholes?"

"Ssht." He guided her toward the council chamber.

"I'm proud of your spirit, but we need their help. If you do much more to piss Eran off, they'll send us packing."

Chloe stopped dead in the middle of a corridor, and then moved until she faced him squarely. "I'm no one's broodmare. Not for any cause including wiping out vampires. Hell's bells, if magic wanes in the world because vampires suck it dry, dragons will suffer along with everyone else."

"You know it; so do I. Let's see if we can convince them."

"Will it just be Eran?"

"Not sure." After the exchange they'd just had in the hallway, he half expected the council chamber would be empty.

They passed the door to the kitchens, so he detoured to pour a tumbler full of the mead-laced nectar the dragons favored and handed it to Chloe. She took a tentative swallow and then a heftier one. "This is good. Thank you."

"You're welcome. Two more doors down on the right."

She turned in where he'd indicated, and he followed her into the dragons' smaller, more intimate meeting room. High ceilinged, it could still accommodate them in wyrm form. Chairs had been moved into a circle with Eran in one and Yahn, second in command, in another. As silver as Eran was gold,

Yahn's hair glistened like gunmetal and his gray eyes held a keen intelligence. Garbed in a dark robe similar to Zee's, he nodded and said in a strong brogue. "Sure and 'tis been a long time, Zachary."

"Too long," Zee agreed. He waited until Chloe sat and then settled next to her.

Eran's expression could have been etched in stone. "I'm listening, Zachary. What ill-fated news accompanies you?"

Chloe set her glass on the floor next to her and began talking. "Everything began with Sarai Lurie, a wolf shifter, and her uncle, Stephan. He's a mountain cat in his other form. In any event, those two and Stephan's wife, Marie, were kidnapped by vampires. They killed Marie, and—"

"I did not ask you." Eran spat the words individually. "In dragon society, women do not forward opinions unless we give them leave."

"My dragon says that's pure hogwash." Chloe stood, facing off in front of Eran with her hands on her hips.

Zee leaned forward, fascinated. Eran would either toss them out on their ear or back down. Chloe had forced his hand, something Zee had never had the balls to do. He'd dealt with conflict by leaving. Not Chloe. Damn but she was one gutsy woman.

"Either sit back down or leave." Eran was on his feet, staring down at Chloe.

"Temper, temper," Yahn said. "I, for one, would hear about a vampire threat if it has, indeed, risen. I saw glimpses of such in my pool."

"Even if the messenger has the unfortunate luck of being female?" Derision lined Chloe's question.

"I would hear from both of you," Yahn said smoothly.

"Good enough." Chloe backed toward her seat and folded into it. "Are you a seer?"

"I am." Yahn bobbed his head.

"We should get you together with Sarai, a wolf shifter with strong psychic ability," Chloe said.

"You never know, dragon"—Yahn stressed the last word—"it just might happen."

Zachary appreciated promising entry points when they presented themselves. Timing was everything in a courtroom too, and now was a perfect opportunity to begin talking.

"As Chloe mentioned," he began, "vampires kidnapped three shifters, killing one of them. Normally, the undead wouldn't have had enough power to manage such a feat, but they located a cadre of willing mages—ones who still hated shifters from our war in the Old Country—and suckered them into sharing their magic..."

Next to him, Chloe picked up her drink. He shot an encouraging glance her way after relating the part where Niall had rescued Sarai and Stephan. "Feel free to chime in whenever you wish."

"Why thank you, I'll do that, but so far you're doing fine."

Her praise warmed him, and he kept on talking.

Chloe had a temper. She'd always been plagued by a short fuse, and her reaction to the sanctimonious piece of shit who saw her as a commodity to be married off to a conveniently single dragon shifter rankled. She probably shouldn't have been so blunt. As she replayed her standoff with Eran, she cringed. Only an hour before, she'd recognized the need to suck up her principles if it meant obtaining help for their cause.

How quickly resolutions could crumble.

She listened carefully as Zee synopsized the hell they'd lived through, adding to his recitation in spots. Hearing everything laid out, one grueling incident on top of the next, made her blood run cold. She'd put her head down and done what needed doing by blocking out what had gone before.

Eran's supercilious expression slipped during Zee's recitation, traded first for disbelief and then dismay. "That's quite a tale," he said after Zee fell silent. "You were right to return to us."

Yahn narrowed his fog-colored eyes to thoughtful slits. "What you said mirrors what I've seen in both my pool and my glass."

Eran twisted to face him. "Why didn't you say something?"

Yahn shrugged, the gesture eloquent. "I was waiting."

"For what?" Chloe spoke up, her tone sharper than she'd meant it to be, but she couldn't take the words back.

"What else?" he countered. "I was biding my time to see if it would become a problem for us."

Zachary's noisy intake of breath was followed by smoke and steam. He got to his feet and strode to where he faced them all. "I'm going to quote Niall, a jaguar shifter, and remind you there is no more us and them. That goes for the shifter mage rift as well as the rift you"—he leveled his gaze at Eran and Yahn—"artificially created between dragon shifters and the rest of our kin."

"Don't waste your breath stating the obvious," Eran growled amid smoke and flames.

"Will you help?" Chloe cut to the chase. If the

answer was yes, it was time to craft plans. If the answer was no, she and Zee needed to get back to the group in Silverthorne.

Magic flashed and flared between Eran and Yahn, and she assumed they were communicating. Zee remained where he was, watching the other two men. She caught his eye, and he motioned for her to join him.

She drained the remainder of the mead mixture coating the bottom of her glass, set it down, and walked to Zachary's side. "We should leave soon," she murmured. Given a choice between telepathy and quiet speech, she figured she had a better chance not being overheard using the latter.

"I know. Give this a few more minutes."

She stood easily next to him. Her magic had recovered quickly, probably with an assist from her dragon, and she felt far better than she had when she'd stumbled through the door of the dragons' stronghold.

"I'd take full credit," her dragon spoke warmly, *"but the drink helped too. It's formulated specially for dragonkind."*

Gratitude blindsided her, and Chloe sent thanks inward. Thanks for believing in her. Thanks for bonding with her. Thanks for sticking up for her when Eran would have turned her into breeding stock.

Puffs of white smoke issued from her mouth.

Zachary smiled. "Your bondmate is happy about something."

Chloe grinned back. "Good. I was just making sure it understood how much I appreciate it."

"That's the recipe for a long and happy bonding," Zee murmured.

"Or for success in any relationship," she replied.

The multihued shroud floating between Eran and Yahn broke into streamers. Eran got to his feet. Yahn followed a beat later. "We will help," Eran said.

"Aye, I fear we have no choice," Yahn added. "The very fabric of Wylde Magick is threatened. If we do not intervene, all that will be left is the Black variety."

"We could continue to bide here," Eran went on, "but eventually this bastion would crumble without Wylde Magick to support it."

"Unfortunately, we'd be next," Yahn cut in dryly.

"Excellent." Zachary moved close and held out a hand. First Eran and then Yahn clasped it. "Our current base of operations is in Silverthorne, Colorado, but we will like as not move to Golddust, a deserted mining town. Easier to escape notice from humans there."

"We can find you, no matter where you are," Eran noted. "Or have you forgotten?"

"Of course I didn't forget," Zee snapped. "I was being polite."

A rolling snort from Yahn was followed by, "We've never valued civility. Sure and you've lived in close quarters with humans far too long."

"Aye, long enough to absorb their deplorable customs." Eran turned his attention to Chloe and softened his tone to compulsion-laden silk. "You'd be safer remaining with us, my dear."

Chloe batted air that had thickened around her. "Stop it. I'll take my chances returning. My friends are there. So is my brother."

"The cave lion?" Eran arched a golden brow.

"The same," she retorted. "I love him, and I'm proud of the beast that picked him for a bondmate." Once the words started, they tumbled out. "I'm proud of my bondmate too, but I don't plan to turn my back on my other shifter friends. We're all in this together. No type of shifter is better than any other, nor are shifters superior to mages. If we can't embrace egalitarian attitudes, we're doomed."

She waited for Eran to shush her, rebuke her for her unsolicited comments, but he simply stared at her speculatively. "You'd be a worthy mate for me, Chloe Fuller." He bowed from the waist. "Will you accept my troth?"

Chloe's mouth fell open. Of all the things he might have said, she'd never, never have guessed at this one.

Next to her, Zachary stiffened. Would he speak up?

Tell Eran off? Redirect him to the problem at hand rather than a misplaced marriage proposal? Silence thickened until she could almost see it hover betwixt them.

She tried out soft refusals, words that wouldn't threaten their brand-new alliance. Before she came up with something gentle, but not too encouraging, Zachary grasped her hand hard enough to hurt.

He addressed his words to Eran while continuing to crush her hand. "Chloe has no way of knowing this since she and I have not discussed our relationship, but I cast first claim to her. I met her first. My dragon proclaimed her as our mate."

"Mine did as well," Eran tossed his head until the jewels woven into his hair clattered against each other. "I'm the elder, so my offer takes precedence."

"The hell it does." Fire shot from Zachary's mouth.

Waves of heat rolled through her, from feet to head and back again. While she was delighted Zachary wanted her, a healthy dose of anger vied for ascendancy. She yanked her hand from Zee's, alarmed to see satisfaction carve into Eran's face.

"Now you look here, both of you." She shook a finger at them and kept her tone stern, businesslike. "I belong to myself." She tapped her breastbone. "I decide who will court me. I decide the if and the when. And this is not the time for mating or courting or however you frame it. We march into battle, *men*." She stressed the word men to shame them. "Let's see who's even standing on the far side of it."

"I forbid you to take part in active conflict," Eran declared. "Our women are too few and too precious to risk."

Chloe rolled her eyes. Rather than ask which century he'd crawled out of, because she had a pretty good idea, she clamped her jaws together to contain her fury before gritting out, "Your efforts to protect me are misplaced. Zachary and I are leaving. Or, at least, I am."

It would be easier—and take far less magic—to teleport to the cave where she'd left her clothes than to fly there. Without waiting for the men, who were still embroiled in a flame-riddled standoff, to say anything, she summoned a transport spell. With the help of her dragon, it formed fast and whisked her out of the dragons' council chamber.

She had no idea if Zee would follow her, but it didn't matter. She didn't require him to get back. She hadn't realized how much more robust her magic was. Between her and her bondmate, they'd make it back to Colorado handily.

"*Nicely done,*" her dragon said.

"*What? All I did was leave. Nothing more to say,*

and if I'd remained I'd have let that Eran fellow have it square between the eyes."

"Come now. He offered us a great honor."

The entrance to the cave where she'd left her things shimmered into being around her, and she hustled inside, letting her borrowed robe drop to the dirt floor. The chilly air cut through her like a knife as she grappled with her clothes.

Chloe reverted to normal speech as she dressed. "Surely, you're not recommending we seriously consider—"

"Nay, I merely wanted you to recognize what an honor his offer is. Eran has been the leader of the dragon shifters for the last thousand years. He seems stiff and formal because of the era he came from, but—"

"I'm not as old as him," Chloe cut in, "but I remember when it was perfectly acceptable for women to be property and not speak until spoken to. He's had centuries to change his ways and has chosen not to. Hell will freeze nine feet thick before I link my life to his."

She laced her boots and zipped her jacket to her chin. Zee wasn't back yet, and she was ready to leave. She'd give him five minutes before heading out on her own.

"If not Eran, what about Zachary?" The dragon had

returned, its tone sly. *"His dragon was ready to mate with us."*

"What? When?" Chloe felt like a fool. Something huge had happened, and she'd missed it.

"After we first arrived and shifted to wyrms." Her bondmate hurried on. *"If we mate in dragon form, we will be bound to him forever, so you must be certain before it happens. I'd have spoken up then, but the others arrived and saved me the trouble."*

Chloe sank to a crouch, hands splayed in front of her for balance. "What other interesting little rules don't I know about?"

"Probably quite a few, but none are as critical as that one."

The scent of Zee's magic blasted her, and she rose, ready to face him. Had he planned to trick her? Have sex with her, and then she'd be stuck? "Would it be the same in human form?" she demanded.

"No," the dragon replied.

Zee strode into the cave, naked, so he must have left his robe back at the dragon stronghold. She tried not to look at the vista of muscled shoulders, flat stomach, and acres of shapely legs, but it was a losing battle. The cock swinging between those wonderful legs nested in a mat of copper curls. She couldn't not look at it, either. It drew her like a lodestone.

"Sorry. I've been trying to get out of there ever

since you left." He flashed a smile her way and stopped dead. "What's wrong? Other than Eran being his usual arrogant self, that is."

Heat suffused her face, but blushing was the least of her problems. "I just heard what it means if we mate as dragons. Were you planning to tell me or just snare me and give me the happy news later?" Her eyes filled with unexpected tears. "Goddammit, Zachary. I was having such a wonderful time flying with you, and you were playing me, planning an aerial seduction. How could you?"

His smile shattered. "I was not playing you. I would never do that. You're important to me. I'd also not have mated with you without making certain you knew what it meant. Christ, woman, what kind of a cad do you take me for?"

He punched the air with a fist and strode to his clothes, grabbing them in handfuls and dressing fast. Somewhere between his shirt and trousers, he said, "If your dragon told you I'd do such a thing, I'd like to talk with it."

Chloe's mouth opened, but it wasn't her voice that emerged. "All I told my bondmate was that your dragon was ready to mate with us, which is a true statement. I challenge you to deny it." The dragon's tone was low, rich, different from how she heard the creature in her mind.

Zee surprised her by bowing low. "Thank you for heeding my request, ancient one. I do not deny my dragon was ready to mate with you. I held it in check because I had to tell Chloe what such an act would mean." He hesitated before adding, "Please tell your bondmate you heard truth in my words."

"Aye, you spoke the truth," the dragon said before relinquishing control of Chloe's vocal chords.

She sputtered at the intrusion and murmured, "What an odd experience."

"And an infrequent one. I didn't expect your bondmate would accede to my request." He zipped his jacket. "We need to leave."

"I was prepared to return on my own."

He leveled blue eyes on her. "About now, I'd be more than happy to tell you to go for it, but I don't want to have to explain to your brother why you never made it back if something goes wrong. Don't worry. I'll make certain to deliver you to Silverthorne, and then I won't bother you further."

A little piece of her heart shredded, followed by another. "I'm sorry. I made assumptions..."

Zachary shook his head. "Those assumptions cast me as a rotter and an insensitive rake who's only out for my own interests."

Magic boiled around them, so strong it almost knocked her off her feet. His travel spell swept them up and away from the cave. She didn't blame him for being angry. She was a master at pushing people away. Why should this relationship—or non-relationship—be any different?

Questing about for a neutral topic, she finally asked, *"What happened with Eran and Yahn?"*

"I wondered when you'd get around to asking. War is your bailiwick. I was a fool to hope for anything else from you."

She cringed. She'd hurt him, and now he was slinging shit her way. *"You didn't answer my question. I'm not asking you to like me, but we have to work together."*

He was silent so long, she feared he wouldn't answer her. His rejection stung, but she'd caused it by assuming the worst of him.

Exactly what I deserve. Buck up and move on.

Brave words. Now all she had to do was put them into action. Emotional strength was one of her assets, and it wasn't as if she'd done more than lust after Zachary from afar. He'd been correct when he told Eran no words had passed between them.

"The dragons will meet us in three days' time." Zachary's voice dragged her from the bleak pit her thoughts had become. *"They will find us wherever we happen to be and have promised at least twenty warriors. Initially, they planned to allocate half that*

number, but I convinced them vampires no longer resided in seethes. They understood the problem better after that."

"Thank you for telling me." She stopped there. She'd already apologized and look how far it had gotten her. Nowhere.

Black shaded to gray, and the travel spell spat them out in her fenced backyard. It was nighttime, and snow sluiced from dark skies. Without a backward glance, Zachary turned and hurried up the steps, leaving footprints in the freshly fallen snow. Magic flashed as he opened the door, and then he was gone.

Chloe stood in the yard, not ready to face anyone. She was confused and ashamed. In a corner of her soul, she was afraid she'd made a mistake there was no recovering from.

"Well, did I?" she asked the dragon, but it didn't respond.

"Oh for the love of Pete, get a grip," she told herself, still talking out loud. Soap opera syndrome had never been her style, and she'd be damned if she'd sink to that level now. She'd been alone forever. It wasn't all that bad. In truth, she'd grown used to it.

Lots of advantages to being on her own, except at the moment she couldn't think of any of them.

Lights flickered on in the kitchen. She trudged up the steps and let herself inside. Zee had already unlocked the door, saving her the trouble. Everyone was gathered around him in the country kitchen with its informal eating space.

"We have three days," he was saying. "During that time, it would help tremendously if we could locate at least a few vampire groups. Places to begin our assault. Maybe if we kill enough of the bastards, they'll pull up stakes and return to New Orleans—or wherever their home base is these days."

"Don't count on it," Stephan said.

Sarai detached herself from Niall's side and came to stand next to Chloe where she leaned against the outside door. "You look like hell." The words were soft and spoken next to her ear.

"Eh, mirrors how I feel."

Sarai hooked a hand under Chloe's elbow and tugged her toward the hallway door. Fortunately, it was at their end of the kitchen.

Chloe followed, not wanting to make things worse by remaining in the same space with Zachary any longer than absolutely necessary. He knew what had transpired with Eran and Yahn. She knew enough. In the days that followed, she'd make certain not to be paired with him on work details.

Sarai walked a few doors down the main hallway and ducked into the library. Once Chloe cleared the lintel, Sarai sent a jot of magic to close the door. "What happened?" she asked without preamble.

"What didn't?" Chloe leaned against a glass-fronted bookcase and sank to her haunches.

"You found the dragons, so why do you look like the face of doom?"

Breath whistled from between Chloe's teeth, mixed with steam and smoke.

Sarai grinned. "Neat trick. Wish I could do that." A howl issued from her throat.

It broke Chloe out of her funk, and she chuckled. "I like your wolf. It just made a statement."

"Indeed, it did. Smoke is overrated. Howling trumps it by a country mile." Sarai laughed too, and then added, "Whatever this is, you'll feel better for sharing it."

"Not sure about that." Chloe raked her hands through hair that had mostly escaped its braids. "There are a lot of dragon shifters. I saw more than fifty. Their leader wants me for his mate."

Sarai shook her head emphatically. "Nope. Zachary is your mate, pure and simple. I've spent enough time with your charts to know that."

"Doesn't matter. I blew that one big time. He's mad—and hurt. Bad combination. Anyway, I managed to extinguish any shred of romance between us." Chloe shrugged. "Maybe it's not a bad thing. We have bigger fish to fry."

Sarai hunkered in front of her and placed her hands on her shoulders. "Agreed about prioritizing the vampire problem, but you can't escape your attraction to Zachary. A shifter's mate is in the stars, sweetie. And he's yours. If you bypass him, you'll never find another man to love."

Sarai stopped long enough to take a breath. "I fought my attraction to Niall but finally gave into it. Same gig. He's my mate, just like Renee and your brother belong together."

"But I was a mage until very recently," Chloe protested.

"Doesn't matter." Sarai grinned crookedly. "Their mates are foretold too. This isn't just about the shifter mate bond. Magic is in play, and everything magical points to you and Zee as forever partners."

She rose, said, "Think about it. Get some rest," and slipped out of the library.

Weariness washed over Chloe in waves. Not wanting to run into anyone else, she teleported to her room two floors up. Bending, she unlaced her boots and pitched facedown on her bed. She was tired, but her mind raced in crazy, disjointed circles.

"Your friend, the wolf, is right," her dragon said.

"Right about what?" Chloe was having a hell of a hard time focusing on anything.

"Zachary is our mate."

"Then why'd you go into all that song and dance about what an honor Eran's proposal was?"

"I was testing you. We're still getting to know one another."

Anger raced to the fore, and she bolted to a sit, fists balled into tight circles. Everyone was manipulating her, and she was done with all of it. "Well, don't."

The spot within her where the dragon resided developed an empty feeling. Crap. Had it left too?

"Fine," she snapped and dropped her legs over the side of the bed, stomach tight and sour with tension. "Go. All of you. I'll get by. I always have."

Her eyes grew hot and gritty; pressure built in her chest. She barely had time to build a ward around herself to muffle sound when sobs pushed out of her. Great, choking gasps that stole her breath and left her feeling hollow and defeated.

She cried for a long time before fatigue claimed her, and she fell into an exhausted sleep.

CHAPTER 9

Zachary teleported home once he was done answering questions. He knew the exact moment when Chloe and Sarai left the kitchen, and he felt Chloe's magic when she moved upstairs, presumably to her room.

Her room.

He wanted to go to her in the worst way but wouldn't let himself. She didn't trust him, and she couldn't hold him in any kind of regard and believe he'd have tricked her by engaging in sex in their dragon forms. Fire belched from his mouth, and he turned aside before a stray cinder landed on the heavy, cream-colored draperies in his study.

Too wound up to sit still, he crossed the hall to the library, but it was a mistake. Her scent lingered on the books she'd left. Breathing it in got his blood going.

"Fuck!" He doubled up a fist and drove it into wooden wainscoting, so spun out he was beyond caring how much his hand hurt.

The others hadn't wanted him to leave, but he couldn't remain beneath the same roof as Chloe. Couldn't.

"You always were one stubborn bastard," the dragon observed.

"At the same time as I'm an arrogant dick or in between times?" Zee's tone was sour, but he wasn't in any mood—for anything. What he should do was return to work. He'd done what he could. Dragons were on their way. Enough of them would arrive, no one would miss him.

Least of all Chloe.

He punched the wall again. Pain shot up his arm this time, and he yelped.

"Stop feeling sorry for yourself," the dragon directed.

"Leave me alone. If it weren't for your incessant meddling, I'd still be in my cozy chambers presiding over cases. I'd never have met Chloe Fuller, and I'd be a hell of a lot happier."

Fire roared from his chest and out his mouth. He stumbled to a window and threw open the sash. Fire kept right on rolling. It melted the metal screen material, but the soaked trees and shrubs weren't in any danger of going up in flames. Smoky tendrils rose from a few spots in the room that had ignited in his mad dash for the window, but he couldn't leave where he stood to stomp them out.

"Stop it." He threw magic behind the command.

The flames ceased, which surprised him. He hadn't expected his bondmate to cooperate. Between his shoes and a towel from the bathroom at the back of the library, he smothered the small infernos. Too bad about the carpet. It was priceless, and now it was marred beyond easy repair.

He slid into a chair and slumped against its back, drained. The carpet didn't matter. Neither did the trivial work he put so much stock in, parading around in his judge robes.

"*You are not returning to your travesty of a job,*" the dragon said. "*I want to make certain we're clear on that.*" When Zee didn't answer, his bondmate went on. "*You like it because people kowtow to you, and it yields a false sense of self-importance. So much so, you almost lost sight of your true self.*"

"Are you quite done?" Zee pushed wearily to his feet.

"*No.*"

"Well, I am. Whatever else you want to say will

have to wait." He hurried from the library, ripe with Chloe's wildflower and cinnamon scent, not wanting to think about her. He'd made a huge mistake letting her into his private world enough to matter.

And now, I have to push her right back out. How hard could it be?

He didn't bother answering himself. It would be damned difficult. She was his mate. He felt the bond in his bones, and she sang to him in a way no other woman ever had. He'd loved his human partner, but that type of love couldn't hold a candle to the passion between two dragon shifters.

Passion that even now scoured his soul to bedrock.

He mounted carpeted risers to his suite of rooms on the top floor, needing to blank out his mind but unable to erase Chloe from his thoughts. His cock swelled again; he'd been perpetually hard since meeting her. Another sign they were fated for one another.

Usually the muted earth tones of his bedroom soothed him, but not tonight. He walked into the marble bathroom and glanced at the green-veined tub but didn't feel like waiting for it to fill. Baths were for relaxing. If his current mood persisted, he didn't think he'd ever chill out again.

He gripped the smooth, cool countertop and regarded his reflection in the mirror that covered the whole wall. A dirt smudge ran across one cheek. His hair stuck up at odd angles. His jacket and pants had spots and were starting to fray, probably courtesy of the long teleport. That type of travel was hard on clothing.

He looked ragged enough, probably no one he worked with at the courthouse would even recognize him. Flipping on the taps, he cupped water in his hands and washed them before bending to sluice more water over his face.

He removed clothing a piece at a time, chucking each down the laundry chute that led to a hamper in the downstairs laundry room. The garments held Chloe's scent too. Smell was the most primitive sense, and the hardest to get away from. Maybe if he added a bleach tablet to the machine, it might expunge the cinnamon and wildflower smell that urged him to teleport into her bed.

"Bad idea. Very bad idea." He shook a finger at his reflection in the glass.

Between bleach and keeping the library door firmly shut, he might have a chance of getting through the three days before the dragons were due to arrive.

A quick trip through the shower, and he headed for bed. The high-thread-count sheets didn't soothe him, though. He reached back and rearranged his pillows. What he needed was sleep. His eyes burned from exhaustion, and his body trod a familiar edge.

One where he was too keyed up to be much good to anyone.

He'd told the assorted mages and shifters at the Silverthorne house he planned to spend the time between now and when the other dragons materialized scouting vampire nests. No one had liked the idea, but he hadn't stuck around for them to badger him out of it.

He worked best alone. Nothing about that had changed.

Why should it?

He was the same dragon shifter he'd always been.

"Bullshit." The word ripped from the bottom of his damaged soul. He feared he'd never be the same, but he couldn't go there. Finding the vampires was paramount. Once found, they could be destroyed, along with any mages unlucky enough to be in proximity.

After all was said and done, he'd pick up the reins of his life and go back to his nice, safe courtroom in the heart of Denver. He loved the old building, and—

"*Think again.*" The dragon's words were cold and clear. "*If you do that, you will be doing it without me. I am done with the half-life where you're more human than shifter, and I have no place at all.*"

Zee tried out a few conciliatory phrases, but his heart wasn't in it. Chloe thought he was an insensitive clod, and the dragon had just threatened to leave. Was this what his life had turned into? A place where everyone he cared about abandoned him?

A low growl rattled from his throat, followed by steam. Vampires first. Everything else took a very distant back seat. When he finally shut his eyes, sleep descended like a hammer, knocking him out cold.

Two DAYS LATER, he was skulking at the borders of a burned-out tenement on the outskirts of Denver. It was high noon, and he wasn't being particularly careful. The vamps he'd found hadn't been all that active during daylight hours, and he hadn't located any mages in proximity to them. He'd always enjoyed field work, and the past few days had almost given him a new lease on life. His dragon hadn't said another word—after threatening to break their bond—and he'd ignored most of the telepathic messages from the other shifters and mages.

He'd shut off his cellphone. The others probably thought he was an insufferable asshole by now, but Chloe already viewed him through that particular lens, and her opinion was the only one that mattered to him.

Not that he could do much about it. He wasn't the flowers-and-candy groveling type. Anger would carry him through this exactly as it had other difficult circumstances.

Time and distance were the final solution. He'd employ both once the vampires were on the run. Perhaps Eran was right, and it was high time for him to return to the flight. At least they understood him, and his dragon would be in favor of such an arrangement.

He'd let Niall and Stephan know the location of the half dozen vampire nests he'd unearthed as soon as he found each one, but he'd cut communication beyond that. They'd just nag him to return to Silverthorne, and he wasn't about to comply. He'd drive most of the way to Golddust later tonight or tomorrow morning and rendezvous with the group. From the sound of things, they'd had some luck as well.

He continued his reconnaissance while running various strategies through his mind. Between all of them, they'd located something like fifteen vampire nests. The problem with finding so many was as soon as they wiped out one, the others would go on high alert. The odds of them staying put were nil. If they had pet mages in the wings, they'd haul them front and center and go into hiding.

And then things would get a whole lot harder fast.

An uncomfortable feeling pricked the base of his neck. He shrank into a conveniently shadowed alcove that had probably once served as a closet and draped himself with subtle magic. Warding didn't do much good if it painted a target on his back, one that screamed, "Here I am."

His nose twitched. The chemical smells of drug manufacture still clung to the shards of wood, all that was left of the closet. No wonder the place had burned to the ground.

He shut his eyes and finetuned his magical senses. Vampires were close. Maybe as many as six or seven, they were below ground, but not far. Perhaps the tenement had a basement. Made sense the fuckers would opt for a spot shielding them from daylight. After the snowstorm, Colorado's abundant sun had returned, and the day was cold but bright and clear.

The rise and fall of voices reached him. Listening in might be instructive, yield insight about what the vampires had planned. *"Can you hear?"* he asked his bondmate. The creature may have adopted a low profile, but it was still part of him.

The muted buzzing broke apart into recognizable words as the dragon shared its superior hearing with Zee.

"I tell you we don't have enough yet," a gravelly voice insisted.

"And I tell you I do not have a good feeling about things. Something is bearing down on us, and we must be readier than we are."

"You always were an alarmist—even when you were still alive," voice number one retorted.

"Your mother fucks donkeys," voice number two muttered.

Zee smothered a snicker. Vampires didn't get along with one another. It wasn't exactly a surprise. They'd been the dregs of humanity when they were alive. Death hadn't improved their dispositions.

"Stuff it," a female voice with sultry overtones jumped in. "How short are we?"

"Short." Voice one was back.

"Aye, we lost fifty-six mages in that Idaho cavern," a new voice with a thick Scottish burr noted. "Not the type of loss ye recover from overnight."

"It hasn't exactly been overnight," the woman sneered. "I've pushed you to get out there, find more of the weak, gullible mages for us, but have you cooperated?"

"Your turn to stuff it, Maeve." Voice two, the donkey-fucking one, was back in the fray.

"Give me numbers," the Scott demanded.

"We've managed to locate seventeen mages, but half of them are reluctant recruits."

The woman, Maeve, dissolved in rough laughter. "Oh so that's what we're calling them now? They ran kicking and screaming when they saw us. The only thing that binds them to us is mesmerism, and I tire of fueling the spell."

"Get over it," voice one growled. "We need their magic. Doesn't matter how we hang onto them, we cannot lose our grip."

"The lot of you are seriously cracked." A man with a British accent slurred the words. He sounded drunk, except vampires only drank blood.

"Aye, and if ye're so brilliant, what's your idea?" the Scott shot back.

"You already know," the Brit countered. "We storm that old house in Silverthorne. Tonight, when our power is strongest. That's where the lion shifter who shit all over our last cache of mages lives. He's also the one who murdered our kin in Transylvania. I tell you, he must be their leader. If we can capture him, the others will be so anxious to bargain for his return, we'll get a free ride. Anything we want. Unlimited blood—"

"Dream on, Chad," donkey fucker cut in. "From what I know of mages, they'd let him rot before they'd offer us anything."

"I say we find out," Maeve spoke smoothly. "We'll visit our captive mages, top off our magic, and show up around midnight. They'll be asleep, not expecting us." The sound of palms slapping together punctuated her words.

"Doona underestimate them," the Scott warned.

Zee had heard plenty. He had to get to Silverthorne and warn everyone. Extricating himself from his current position wouldn't be easy, though. He'd shrouded his brand of magic in bits and pieces of the half-rotted multiplex. The minute he moved away from his spot, the vamps might notice something had changed.

"We could teleport." The dragon breathed the barest suggestion of words into his mind.

"No, we can't. The burst of magic will surely draw their attention, and then they'll know they've been overheard, and all my good work eavesdropping will be for naught. We can set a trap for them tonight, now we know they're coming."

"But the other dragons won't be here yet."

"They'll come if I alert them." Zee wasn't at all sure it was true, but he wasn't about to delve into the ins and outs of why Eran would—or wouldn't—heed his request. Chloe lay between them. Eran had thrown down a gauntlet, staked a claim to her. She hadn't quite refused him, merely put him off. Eran was conceited enough, he probably thought she was playing hard to get.

Zachary ground his teeth. He had to focus. He'd done pretty well keeping Chloe out of his mind these past two days. Right now, he had a problem. Escape was paramount. Losing himself in longing for a woman who didn't want him would be worse than stupid.

Modulating both breath and magic, he let go of his warding in tiny bits, waiting for long moments after each alteration. The vampires' conversation continued, their voices rising and falling. It was his bellwether. If they quit talking, or someone asked, "What was that?" he'd have to move even slower.

He willed himself to patience, never his long suit, and slowed his breathing still more. Two more moves, and his warding would be down. Then he could slither from his hiding place—he hoped.

He had to warn the others. Maeve was right about them being asleep in the middle of the night, and a stealth vampire attack could do a lot of damage. Chloe would put her life on the line protecting her brother, and he couldn't let anything happen to her. Even if she didn't want him, had rejected him out of hand, the mate bond ran hot and strong. He'd protect her, shield her, make certain no harm befell her.

He withdrew a short iron blade from a thigh sheath. Not the greatest defense in his current circumstances but striding through downtown Denver carting a medieval saber wasn't practical.

His compromise had been the six-inch blade with a wicked-looking serrated edge. The weapon had been forged with silver and iron. Its handle was stone worn smooth from many generations of dragon shifters wielding it. Stone mitigated the enervating effects of both silver and iron, offering him an advantage and allowing him to wield it without draining his own magic.

He waited through a few more minutes after releasing the magic surrounding him. Satisfied he'd been as thorough as he could, he scanned the immediate vicinity. A few people were scattered along the alleyway behind the tenement. Most sprawled in a drug- or alcohol-induced stupor. A few hunched over cellphones.

He set his jaw in a tight line. What kind of world was it when humanity had devolved into nothing more than staring at a display? The answer depressed him, and he plotted a course. From his hidey hole to the end of the alley, and thence to his car.

Blade at the ready, he abandoned the spot he'd stood for the last hour. He moved slowly, weaving a bit as he tried to blend in with the resident addict population. He put five feet between himself and the subterranean vampire enclave, and then ten. When the distance grew to fifteen, he let himself move a little faster.

He was almost at the end of the alley that stank of piss and vomit when one of the bums rolled to his feet, light and lithe. The stench of vampire hit Zee full in the face. He resisted the urge to gag. Vampires smelled far worse than unwashed humans.

The vamp danced in front of Zee, blocking his exit.

Zee eyed him. "You must be the sentry, old chap."

"You might say that." The vampire raised his upper lip, displaying fangs. Dark hair framed his face, and he pinned Zee with a pair of striking hazel eyes, no doubt expecting to leech his will. Just before he turned him into a midafternoon snack.

Zee watched him dispassionately, knife hidden by his side in folds of his jacket.

"Watch me," the vampire murmured, silky smooth. "Just keep your eyes on me, and all will be well."

"Now, why would I want to do a silly thing like that?" Zee inquired, enjoying the confused look that washed across the vampire's classically handsome face. One of the biggest jokes in the universe was how beautiful vampires were.

"Beautiful and deadly," the dragon spoke up. Smoke slithered from between Zee's lips, followed by a small gout of flame.

"What the fuck?" The vampire drew back.

Zee anticipated him, though, and drove forward, using the vampire's backward motion to shove him to the pitted pavement. The vamp was strong, but no match for a dragon shifter. Zee plunged the dagger into the vamp's throat while the creature raked long, jagged nails down his face. Blood pulsed from severed jugulars, and then carotids, and Zee sawed the blade back and forth.

If he'd had a second blade, he'd have stabbed at the thing's hands. Blood ran down his face from multiple cut places, but so far he'd avoided the vamp's efforts to put out his eyes.

Breath heaved from him as he sat atop the vamp, chopping through bone, sinew, flesh, and vessels. His blade might be sharp, but cutting off heads was a job for a saber, not a hunting knife.

"Good enough," the dragon shouted. *"Run. And then teleport."*

Zee trusted his bondmate, had trusted it for hundreds of years. They'd had a falling out, but none of that mattered. He sprang from the dying vampire with blood sheeting off him and sprinted for the end of the alley. If a cop saw him, he was dead meat.

No way could he stumble through an explanation about running into a wild pig or a deer or something big that could have doused him in blood—and clawed the shit out of his face. Plus, he stank like nobody's business. Nothing wild would have that rank an odor.

He felt vampires behind him. Probably the entire group he'd listened in on. Damn. Did that mean they'd alter their plans? Or would they see him as just one more vampire hunter out for the generous bounty offered for their hides.

Humans hated vampires too, and shows like *Supernatural* had highlighted their existence.

If he teleported—with its accompanying jolt of Wylde Magick—he'd blow the bounty hunter theory right out of the water. He left the alley, feinted right, and ran fast while sprinkling don't-look-here enchantments around him. Humans might not see him, but they shied out of his path, noses crinkling in disgust.

At the next corner, he risked a glance the way he'd come. The street was empty. Must have been too much daylight outside the alley for the vamps to follow him. His car was only a couple blocks away, but he didn't want to sit in it drenched in vampire blood and reeking of death and rot.

"Teleport!" the dragon shrieked. *"Now before they gin up stronger magic and follow us."*

Zee opened his magic to a transport spell. It jumped to his command, probably because the dragon was helping. Moments later, the streets of Denver fell away, replaced by the fenced backyard of the Silverthorne house.

Chloe and Renee were hanging wet laundry on a line. Both of them converged on him. "Talk about a dramatic entrance." Renee shook her head. "Where the fuck have you been? The men have been trying to contact you for days."

"I've talked with them," he protested and looked around for a garden hose. Anything he could rinse off with.

"Yes, but not much," Chloe countered. "Jeremiah's been pissed and worried too." She wrinkled her nose. "Ick. Vampire. Will they be hot on your heels?"

Anger surged at her lack of faith, but she'd asked a fair question and he ran herd on his temper, reining it in. "I hope not. I did my damnedest to not draw them after me. Reason I'm such a mess is I killed one with this." He brandished the bloody blade. "Point me to water. I stink so bad I can't stand myself."

"Drop your clothes out here," Renee said. "We'll shovel them into the washing machine. You can run inside and take a shower. One of the men will have something you can put on."

Zee cast a sidelong glance at Chloe, the last person he wanted to strip in front of. What if his cock got the better of him?

Renee snapped her fingers. "Come on, ace. We haven't got all day."

"No," he agreed, "we don't. Unless the vamps I was eavesdropping on figure out I was something other than a garden-variety bounty hunter, they'll show up here tonight."

Chloe's generous mouth split into a feral grin. "I like it. We'll be ready for them, eh?"

"You bet," Renee said. "And with something better than that puny knife. Oberon's balls, you must have sawed and chopped and hacked to get the thing's head off."

"You have no idea." Zee decided he didn't care about Chloe staring at him. He had to get some distance between himself and his stinking, reeking clothes. Staring with his jacket, he stripped, leaving everything in a pile.

Renee narrowed her eyes. "There's so much blood on you, it's hard to sort things out, but the vamp gored your face, didn't he?"

"Yeah, but it's superficial. Once I'm clean, I'll set magic to patching myself up."

"I could look at the wounds."

He remembered she was a healer. "Kind of you, but I'm sure I'll be fine. Sure you don't want me to carry all that stuff inside?" he asked and pointed to his stack of blood-saturated clothing.

"We're good," Chloe looked him up and down in a frank appraisal he couldn't interpret. "We'll use magic to move them to the washing machine."

"Get inside," Renee instructed. "It's cold out here, and you're naked."

"Thanks for telling me," he replied through teeth

that were beginning to chatter. "I'd never have noticed, otherwise."

"The original funny man." Chloe's eyes were still glued to him, and he felt his anatomy respond to her forthright stare. Before his cock shot to attention, he turned and made for the back steps, intent on putting the first-floor bathroom door between himself and temptation.

CHAPTER 10

"Well? Why are you standing there looking thunderstruck?" Renee punched Chloe lightly in the shoulder.

She shook herself from head to toe, realizing she'd been staring at the spot Zachary had vanished into the house. His body was so incredible—all hard muscles and pleasing lines—it had been impossible not to look. "Sorry," she mumbled, feeling like a kid who'd just seen a guy naked for the first time. Embarrassed by how obvious her interest must be, she hustled to their laundry basket and grabbed a towel and a couple of clothespins.

Renee wrestled the towel out of her hands. "I'll finish up here, and I'll get Zee's clothes going in the machine. Go."

Chloe gave up and let go of the towel. "Go where?"

Confusion reigned, but it might be because her brain had turned to a slushy mix of regret and desire. She'd blown her chance with Zachary, and all the lusting in the world couldn't fix what she'd shattered in a few seconds of thoughtless confrontation.

Renee tossed the towel over the line, securing it with pins in case it got windy, and turned to face Chloe. "Inside. Where else? You two are made for each other. Sarai gave me the lowdown on her astrological findings, although much of it was way over my head. Bottom line: he's your mate. For whatever reason, he dropped into our laps, and—"

"He was running from vampires. Where else would he go?" An image of his lacerated face smote her, and she added, "Do you really think his face will heal without antibiotics or something?"

A squawk rumbled from Renee, sounding suspiciously like her eagle bondmate. "Oh my god, sister. You've got it bad. We have magic. We don't require antibiotics or much of anything in the way of Western medical intervention." She leaned closer, a wicked gleam in her eye. "He's already naked. Be shameless about this."

Heat raced from Chloe's chest and over her head, adding to her arousal. She gave her body a stern command to stand down, goddammit. "You don't get it." She bit off the words. "He doesn't want me. It's why he hightailed it out of here the night we returned from the dragons' stronghold. He can't bear the sight of me. He—"

"Uh-uh. None of that." Renee cut into Chloe's tirade. "You had a lovers' spat. You were hurt, misinterpreted something, and lashed out. He got his scales ruffled." She shrugged. "It happens. Now, hustle inside and make things right."

"What if I can't?" Chloe wrapped her arms around herself, suddenly cold. The thought of laying herself bare and being rejected unnerved her. The humiliation would leave lasting scars.

Which is precisely why I'm alone, an implacable inner voice pointed out, pausing before adding, *Coward.*

Renee turned both hands palms up. "One thing is certain, you'll never know unless you try. Jer and I had our rough spots. I thought he hated me—until he sought me out and made his interest clear."

"Jeremiah is sweet and kind and funny and generous," Chloe muttered.

"What makes you think Zachary doesn't share some of those traits?" Renee furled her brows. "You're stalling, sister."

"Just what I was about to add." The dragon's voice surprised her. It hadn't had anything much to say since the night they returned from Siberia.

Her heart sped up, and her mouth was suddenly dry. "All right." She blew out a tight breath. "Here's hoping I don't fuck this up as badly as I did when I challenged him about the dragon mating ritual."

"That's the spirit. Almost." Renee grinned crookedly. "You've missed him. How about assuming he missed you too, that he longs for you and has only been keeping himself away by exercising gobs of self-discipline."

Chloe waved her to silence. "Enough. I'm going, already." Before she could talk herself out of it, she crossed the yard and mounted the steps to the kitchen porch. Already beating fast, her heart edged up a few more notches, thundering in her chest. Waves of heat alternated with blasts of cold. Once she was in the kitchen, which was mercifully empty, she took a few deep breaths to pull herself together.

What was she going to do?

Walking into the bathroom where she heard the shower running seemed like a huge violation of his privacy. But if she waited until he was done, he'd be embroiled in plans for later this evening. Maybe if enough vampires showed up, they'd knock a hole in their ranks big enough to discourage them for a while.

Or maybe not.

Jeremiah had mowed through twenty vamps in

Transylvania without any appreciable decrease in their activity.

"What are you waiting for?" the dragon prodded.

"A staunch dose of courage."

The shower noise ceased. It was now or never. Either she did this or skulked upstairs and shrouded herself in her insular cocoon, surrendering to her fears.

"I'm better than that," she told the empty kitchen and marched through it and into the hallway. The bathroom was one door down. Just opening the door and stepping inside felt truly intrusive, so she raised her fist and knocked.

A blast of magic raked her and was withdrawn so fast she was certain her presence was a shock. He'd been checking who wanted in, never expecting she'd be outside his door.

Chloe forced herself to stand her ground, breathing around the narrow space her throat had become. He'd either let her in or tell her to fuck off. Either way, she had to see this through. Minutes dripped past, but she'd be damned if she'd back down. He knew she was still outside the door.

Finally, the latch snicked open. Steam rolled into the hall. Chloe stared at the open door. Was it an invitation?

Christ! I'm pathetic.

Squaring her shoulders, she walked inside and shut

the door behind her. Zachary had wrapped a towel around his waist. Newly washed hair hung to the middle of his chest, even brighter than when it was dry. The clawed places in his face were still obvious but looked like they were healing.

He skewered her with his implacable gaze and quirked one ruddy brow. "What was it that couldn't wait until I was decent?"

Chloe ripped her gaze from the muscles bunching across his shoulders and along his arms where he'd crossed them over his chest. He was so striking he stole her breath and her wits.

She opened her mouth, but it was so dry, only a croak emerged. Swallowing hard, she tried again. "We got off onto a wrong foot, you and me. I wanted to apologize. What I said in the cave was wrong. I made assumptions I shouldn't have, and I'm very sorry. I—" The next words huddled in the safety of her throat, but she booted them out the gate. "I like you. Admire you. Respect you." Heat suffused her cheeks until she had to be bright red.

His chiseled lips—lips she'd love to kiss—twitched at their corners, and he made come-along motions with one hand. "You're doing great, wench. Keep it coming."

"Aren't you going to say anything? Yell at me and agree I was a mouthy bitch?" Still unsure of her reception, she retreated to questions.

"I have no plans to yell at you. Beyond that, who wouldn't enjoy hearing their virtues extolled?" His eyes crinkled at the corners, and he opened his arms. "Come here, Chloe."

Wordlessly, she crossed the small space and walked into his embrace. When he locked his hands behind her, she leaned into him and threw her arms around his naked back. The touch of his skin beneath her fingertips was electric with promise, and tingles shot to her breasts and the dark, secret place between her legs.

He threaded his fingers through her hair and just held her for long, delicious moments. His scent, the one she craved, bloomed around them until the bathroom smelled like the Scottish Highlands after a spring rainstorm.

"I'm sorry too." His deep voice buzzed against her ears. "I'm too arrogant for my own good, and I shouldn't have ridden off into the sunset on my high horse. I pride myself on my equanimity, but you unbalanced me. You were all I could think about, and how you viewed me was important. So important, I overreacted all over the place at the merest hint you didn't believe I was perfect."

"I don't blame you." Her words were muffled against his chest.

"Aye, but I blamed myself, once I got past my initial fury when I condemned you for not recognizing what a stellar fellow I am." He stroked her head, holding it in the hollow between his neck and shoulder. "Dragon shifter customs are brand new to you. I should have been more compassionate, more empathic. Instead, I went off on a tear, assumed you'd scrutinized me through a cracked lens—and not in any good ways."

She nestled closer; desire spilled through her in waves, mingled with relief he hadn't sent her packing. "Does this mean we get to start over?"

"Sweetheart." He turned her head, tilting her face upward. "We never started at all." His lips were hot, sweet, urgent as he closed them atop hers. She clung to him, kissing him back as if he was the only solid thing in her world. Their lips crashed together, parted, and collided once more. Kisses turned to bites and suckles, and then back to kisses.

Her nipples formed peaks where they pressed against his chest, and she felt his cock rise in a column, jutting into her belly. She snaked a hand between their bodies and curved her fingers around his ridged flesh. The towel was between them, but it didn't mute his delight at her touch. He made a wonderfully male sound, and his cock jerked in her hand. She explored him, at first trying to get beneath the towel, and then not worrying about it. He was brilliantly endowed. Long, thick, hot, beautiful. She'd bet anything his penis was as gorgeous as the rest of him.

He licked the seam between her lips, and she opened her mouth to his searching tongue. Lust speared her, turning her insides molten as every drop of moisture in her body headed south and pooled between her legs.

Zee's hands trailed across her back and lower until he cupped her ass, snugging her against his erection still trapped in her hand. Her breath, already fast, quickened still more. She wanted so many things. To drop onto her knees and take him into her mouth. To tug her trousers down and bend over the sink so he could plumb her from behind. Each erotic image seeded three more until they formed a sensual kaleidoscope, and her clit beat like a second heart. She rubbed her thighs together, upping the sensation rioting through her.

He ripped his mouth from hers and smiled down at her, his expression filled with possession—and promise. "Is this a sufficient fresh start?" Playfulness lined his words. She'd never have guessed he had a lighthearted side.

She ran her tongue over her swollen lips and teased back, "Maybe. But I need a more extensive sample."

"Oh, darling. So do I, but we have to plan for tonight. If I take you to bed, we'll never leave." Fires smoldered in the depths of his eyes, turning them midnight dark. "Our first time will not be standing up in a steamy bathroom. I want to undress you slowly, worship each bit of flesh I uncover."

"We must fly," blasted from her mouth, courtesy of her dragon. Chloe waited to see if her bondmate had further use for her vocal chords, but it relinquished control.

"I'm not exactly used to that," she murmured, "but it's not as big a surprise as it was the first time."

Zachary's grin widened. "We will take to the skies. Never fear. My dragon is lobbying from the sidelines too." He cupped the side of her face in a broad, calloused hand. His smile evaporated, replaced by a serious expression. "Knowing what you do about mating in dragon form, are you willing to fly with me? Assumptions were almost our undoing, so this is one place we must be absolutely clear with one another." He stopped long enough to take a breath. "For dragonkind, flying together is the equivalent of total commitment. A marriage without divorce where we will be together forever."

His words sent a thrill to the pit of her stomach. She hadn't ruined everything. He still wanted her. "Yes," she replied. "I understand. It will seal us together, formalize the mate bond."

"Aye. If ye need more time"—the lilt of Scotland was back in his speech—"I'll wait forever for you. Och, mayhap not so long as all that, but ye needn't feel rushed into a decision."

Chloe matched his solemnity. For once, she was going to grab what she wanted with both hands. No second-guessing. No hiding behind trivial excuses like not knowing him long enough. "I would be honored to fly with you and become your mate." Her throat, already thick with desire, nearly closed from the emotion spilling through her.

He bent forward and kissed her forehead and both cheeks. When he straightened, a soft smile added an ethereal aspect to his beauty. "You've made me a very happy man." He butted his hips against hers.

"I'm pretty happy, myself." Chloe rolled her eyes. "Sheesh. I've spent most of the time since you ran out of here as if Satan's horde was on your heels kicking myself. I tried to reach you, but you turned off your cell and didn't respond to telepathy. My dragon urged me to go after you, but I figured you didn't want to be found—and there was plenty of work to be done here locating vampire enclaves."

"I'd love to say I tried to contact you"—he glanced away—"but pride got the better of me. My bondmate has told me over and over what an arrogant dick I am. This time, the only thing it did was threaten to break our bond if I returned to work."

Chloe's eyes widened. "Aw shit. Does that ever

happen?" Loyalty and protectiveness for her newly formed bond with her own dragon welled. "I would die if my dragon left, and we barely know one another."

"Not often. There are a scant handful of instances where bond animals walked away from their shifter mates." He nuzzled her neck before reaching down and untangling her hand from his erection. "If you don't let go, it will never go down, and I'll be stuck in this bathroom forever."

Rising on tiptoes, she cradled his head between her hands and kissed him full on the mouth. She tried to imbue everything she was feeling into the touch of her lips against his. Delight. Love. Hope for their future together. Relief her faux pas hadn't been their death knell. Excitement at the prospect of peeling back layers until she knew every centimeter of him, heart, body, and soul.

When she finally let go, he said, "Lovely thoughts, darling. The same goes for me. Let me get dressed. Could you gather everyone in the dining room? I'll be there in a flash."

"Of course." Her body still hummed from his touch and the realization it was only the barest of beginnings. They'd make love soon, and they'd have all the years of their long lives to enjoy one another.

"Very long lives, indeed." He winked.

"What? Are you living inside my head?"

"You bet," he shot back. "Better get used to it."

Chloe floated out of the bathroom. Bliss leaked from her, forming a veritable shroud of delight. She put out a telepathic call for the others as she made her way to the dining room on the far side of the ground floor.

Sarai and Renee showed up first. Renee swept her into a hug. "See? It all worked out?"

"How could it not?" Sarai demanded, adding, "I'm happy for you."

"But I never said anything," Chloe protested.

"You didn't have to," Renee replied. "Joy is sheeting from you in waves. Bliss like that can't be faked."

"Besides"—Sarai offered a knowing smile—"my charts are never wrong. A shifter's mate—"

"Is in the stars," Renee and Chloe chanted as a unit.

Sarai clapped her hands together. "Excellent. I've taught you well, Padawan."

They were still laughing when everyone else trooped into the dining room.

"What's up? Why are we here?" Jeremiah asked. His gaze settled on his sister, and he smirked. "Aha. Got things squared away with the other dragon, eh?"

Chloe made a show of examining herself from head to toe. "What? Have I suddenly turned transparent?"

"Only to all of us who know you." Stella exchanged a knowing grin with Raul.

Zachary swept into the room, wet hair trailing down his back and shoulders and the scars on his face resolving to pale-pink scratches. He trotted to Chloe and wrapped an arm around her shoulders. "Before we get onto the war council part of today, I'm delighted to announce Chloe has accepted my troth. She will become my mate as soon as we can formalize our bond."

Cheers and clapping rang out, along with an, "It's about time," from Jeremiah.

Zachary eyed him. "Planning to come after me with a shotgun, were you?"

"Something like that. Chloe's been looking like someone ripped her heart out, and I figured you had to be the cause." He extended a hand, and Zachary shook it. "No hard feelings. Welcome to the family."

"Thank you. We have work to do, folks. Take a seat." He waited until everyone was sitting, and then strode to the head of the table. "Earlier today, I was out hunting vampire nests like the rest of you. I came across a group literally beneath my feet and hid myself, listening. Unless I screwed things up by killing the sentry—and I may have—they're planning to converge on this house tonight."

A collection of outraged groans surged around the room.

"Better for us to know," Stephan said. "We'll be ready for them."

"Why this house in particular?" Raul asked.

"They recognize Jeremiah as the one who burned their pet mage collection to a cinder," Zee replied. "They also know about the group he wiped out with poison in the Old Country."

"Makes sense." Jeremiah narrowed his eyes. "They'd view me as a ringleader and want to rid themselves of me."

"Nay. They planned to kidnap you, use you as a bargaining chip," Zachary corrected him.

"While they work on ways to siphon my magic." Jeremiah made a sour face. "I'll die before I help them."

"No one is dying on my watch." Renee placed a hand firmly over her mate's.

"How many vamps?" Stephan asked.

"I'm not sure," Zee replied. "At least half a dozen were kicking ideas around, but there could have been more who weren't motivated to take part in the discussion."

"Vampires hold to a hierarchy," Johnny said. "If they're harboring newly made ones, they'd not have yet earned the right to speak freely."

Chloe hadn't known that. She bet there was a whole lot she didn't know about vampires, but it was too late to study up on them between now and tonight.

"I've put out a telepathic call to the dragons," Zachary went on, "requesting they quicken their timeline. It's only a few hours difference, so I'm expecting at least some will show up."

"We need to collect all the iron blades," Jeremiah said. "If the goddess is good to us, we'll have enough so each of us has one."

"Dragons have no need of iron in our wyrm bodies," Zachary said. "We're one creature that can kill with fire."

"My cave lion did a credible job biting off heads." Jeremiah angled a pointed look at Zee.

"Excellent, so we will require three fewer blades," Zachary said, and then added, "If we run short, I have quite a collection at home. I can teleport there and back quickly and return with enough to arm everyone."

"I'll get the blades together," Jeremiah said. "Meet me in the living room in a quarter hour. We'll parcel them out and decide how to best defend this house."

Chloe looked from her brother to her almost-mate. Jeremiah had grabbed the point, but Zachary wasn't fighting him for it. No doubt, he recognized—and respected—her brother's position in their group.

Jeremiah stood and strode from the room. The others moved more slowly, talking among themselves.

Zachary walked the length of the table until he stood by her side and offered an arm. "Shall we?"

Chloe waited until the others had left before saying, "The more time I spend around you, the more I appreciate you."

He snorted. "I'm a real standup guy when my panties aren't in a bunch."

She slugged him playfully. "I'm going to detour through the basement. Your clothes must be done by now, and I'll toss them in the dryer."

"Thanks, but you don't have to wait on me."

"I'm not turning into your valet, just being practical." She switched gears and gave voice to a fear that had dogged her as they'd uncovered one vampire nest after another. "When did there get to be so many vampires?"

"Are you asking how they grew from something we never thought about to their current proportions?" At her nod, he went on. "One vamp at a time. We weren't paying attention, and it offered them a whole lot of latitude."

"Mmph. Not a mistake we're likely to make again."

"Nope, but I fear we'll be living with the fallout from this one for a long time to come."

"What do you mean?" She closed her teeth over her lower lip.

"When we solicited aid from other dragonkind, I had no idea how big the problem was. In truth, I still don't. But my initial strategy, which was to strike fast and hard and obliterate them, will never work."

She nodded and tucked a hand beneath his arm. "Same thing occurred to me. They're not going to remain where we found them, waiting for us to mow them down like a pack of misbehaving dominoes."

He closed his hand over hers and guided them out of the dining room. "One step at a time. Let's see how tonight goes, and then we'll determine what happens next. Eran and Yahn are old beyond reckoning. I bet they'll have some wisdom to share that will help us pick a path."

She grimaced. "Eran. Will he be furious with us?"

Zachary shook his head. "Dragons are a funny lot. Once one of us is spoken for, they're off limits. He only wanted you because you were available." He cleared his throat. "When you've been a dragon longer, you'll feel the hoard hunger, and you'll want to collect things too. Any item not otherwise spoken for is fair game."

"Sounds like I escaped a speeding bullet."

"Not really. He'd have treated you fairly." Zee stopped and turned her to face him. "But he wouldn't have longed for you, loved you like I do."

Before she could respond, he crushed his mouth over hers in a hot, quick kiss that brimmed with possibilities. Still aroused from their skirmish in the bathroom, she jammed her body up against his. They were both flushed and panting when he released her.

To avoid pushing him into the nearby pantry and divesting him of the clothes he'd just donned, she said, "Next time, we finish this."

He winked. "Nay, lassie-mine. Next time, we'll love one another until passion wrings us dry. And then, we'll start all over again. There'll be no finishing. Not that I can see."

His words kindled her imagination, and she fled to the basement stairs with images of him naked cascading through her mind.

His laughter, warm and contented, followed her. "Ye can run, but ye canna hide. Not anymore. Ye're mine."

"Goes double back at ya," she called over a shoulder.

"*When are we flying with him?*" her dragon demanded.

"After the vampire attack tonight." Chloe reached the bottom stair and hustled into the laundry area.

"*Mating is far more important than vampires.*" The dragon sounded indignant.

Chloe bent to switch Zee's wet clothing from

washer to dryer and hunted for an explanation the dragon might understand. "These are my kinfolk," she said. "They need our help—mine and Zachary's—tonight. If something bad happens to any of my friends and I'm not there to do everything I can—"

"*I understand,*" the dragon cut her off. "*Do not make me wait too long, though. He is ours.*"

Chloe liked the sound of *ours.* It made her smile, and she was still grinning like a fool as she took the steps two at a time to join everyone in the living room.

CHAPTER 11

Zachary cleared snow away from his sector of the roof. They'd split up the house, so it would be fully protected from all sides. He'd rather Chloe remained safe in her bedroom, but of course she'd told him to pound sand—after she accused him of being just like Eran. That last had stung. Wrapped in a black hooded parka that hid her bright hair, she sat next to him where two of the gabled roof sections formed a flat place.

Ten dragons had materialized around seven, just about the time Zee returned with three more iron sabers. After totally recrafting everyone's original strategy, the dragons had split into groups and settled along the rooftop. The other shifters and mages were assigned to key locations within, except for Renee.

Since her bondmate could fly, it made sense for her to draw roof duty.

Midnight had long since passed, and it was pushing one in the morning. Zee wondered—again—if the vamps had changed their minds after the untimely death of their sentry. He'd replayed the scene in the alley many times and come up with the same answer. There'd been no way to avoid killing the vampire, not without revealing what he was to the rest of them. It had stood square in his path, intent on draining him.

If he'd shifted, the jig would have been up. Or summoned teleport magic from the alley. If the vampires were suspicious, they might have figured out he wasn't human, but maybe they'd been so suffused in fury about their fallen comrade, they hadn't bothered to look too closely.

Footsteps pattered across the steep roof, and Renee joined them, a saber trailing from her right hand. "Eran wants to know how long we're going to wait."

Zee frowned. The dragons had forbidden telepathy —or any magic at all—not wanting to tip off the vampires they were laying for them. He quashed a desire to snap at Renee, but she was only a messenger. If Eran had questions, he should have come himself.

"As long as you're here, you can wait with us," Chloe said and scooted closer to the gable's edge.

"Thanks." Renee settled next to her. "I appreciate

the dragons coming and all that, but what a dour, short-tempered bunch. If Eran wants to talk with Zachary, he can show up himself." She rolled her eyes. "If he yells at me for not doing his bidding, my bondmate will probably force a shift and peck his eyes out."

Her words about dragonkind pained Zee, but they were true, and he didn't shush her. "It's not exactly an excuse," he mumbled, "but this is probably the first time they've left their stronghold in at least a hundred years, perhaps double that. They've done what all isolated groups do and painted the rest of the world as flawed."

"Um, yeah. That part came through loud and clear." Renee's nostrils flared. "Maybe this will be good for them."

Zee doubted it. His kin were a stiff-necked bunch.

A shadow flickered across his visual field, but was gone so quickly, he might have imagined it. He stared into the darkness, borrowing liberally from his dragon's night vision. "Did you see that?" He kept his words low enough to be at the threshold of the women's hearing.

Chloe and Renee shook their heads, but both leaned forward, scanning the inky black night. No moon, and most of the stars were hidden beneath a thick cloud bank. The air was thick and cold and damp. Snow felt imminent.

He wanted to pay out subtle threads of magic, but

they'd agreed on no magic at all—until they were in the thick of things. The dragons had maintained they'd have the best chance if they waited until the last possible moment to reveal themselves.

Then they could snare the vamps.

Up close and personal.

A heated argument had ensued. Some wanted to ward the house. Others lobbied for a magic-imbued perimeter masquerading as strings of holiday lights. It was late enough in the season, some houses were already decorated. In the end, the dragons had prevailed. With all magic cloaked to nothing, they'd wring every last bit of advantage out of the darkness.

More footsteps, heavier ones. Eran ran across the pitched roof as if it were flat and landed lightly on a small space one gable over. He motioned to Zee, who joined him. To forestall complaints or pointed commentary about how he'd screwed things up by killing the sentry, he bent close to Eran's ear. "We should wait until daylight. We're already in position."

"Same conclusion I came to," the flight leader growled, "although why that bird shifter didn't return to her post is—"

"She doesn't report to you," Zee was quick to remind Eran. "The world is a vastly changed place from when you left it."

"We did not leave."

Zachary locked gazes with him. "What you did amounts to the same thing. Earth has suffered for a lack of dragon magic, but 'tis a topic for another time."

Eran's head snapped up; his nostrils flared as he scented the air. A grim smile split his austere features. "They're coming. Finally. Gods but I've missed bloody, scrappy battles. I'm off to alert everyone." He scrambled up the roof, boot soles sticking to it like glue.

Zee sniffed and stared, but neither eyes nor nose yielded any clues. Eran had sounded certain, though, and he wasn't one to imagine an enemy just because he lusted after conflict. A semi-awkward leap landed him next to Chloe and Renee.

"Get ready." He breathed the words.

"I keep feeling something," Chloe said.

"Me too." Renee nodded. "But it's elusive. There and then not."

He wanted to shield Chloe with his body, but then he'd block her view. He settled for standing in front of both women until they got to their feet and shoved him aside.

The air grew heavy with more than imminent snow. When the stench of death and rot rose out of nowhere, he knew Eran had been spot on. Vampires were closing, but how many and how soon remained to be seen. "Don't call magic yet," he cautioned.

"Got it," Chloe snapped.

"Damn but I hate those fuckers," Renee snarled.

Zachary was surprised they hadn't targeted her. Renee had outsmarted them, let them believe she'd been captured and then sweet-talked them into a flying demonstration...

Crap! Fuck! Damn! He'd almost forgotten some of the undead could fly. The older ones dropped out of the skies like goddamned, perverted bats and scared the living hell out of their targets. Some died of fright before the vamp even latched onto their necks. At least they had back in the Old Country when people were still superstitious.

His skin prickled unpleasantly, and the odor of carrion lying too long under a hot sun thickened. Decaying flesh didn't match up with the ambient air temperature, which had to be in the mid-teens.

"Tough to sneak up on anyone when you smell like that," Chloe muttered.

"If we were asleep, we probably wouldn't notice," Renee said, followed by a startled intake of air.

Zachary followed the line of her gaze in time to see a portal surrounded by black flames form twenty feet or so above their aerial perch. Vampires, the flying variety, poured through the opening. Where he'd expected ten or twelve, the vampires had apparently missed his memo. Twenty blasted through the unnatural slash in the ether, followed by at least that number more.

He stopped counting. In the next few seconds, the vamps would notice them—and all the other shifters arrayed along the old Victorian's gabled roofline. Dragons bugled, and the sky lit with dragon fire.

"It's time," he told the women.

"I'll teleport to where Jeremiah is," Renee said. "Too many vamps on the wing, and I want to be able to wield my blade."

"We'll drive them down to you." Chloe smiled grimly. "It's a promise."

"Perfect." The spot Renee had stood developed a liquid, glistening aspect, and she was gone.

Chloe had stripped while she was talking. Magic bubbled around her as her dragon formed.

He started to shuck his clothes, but his dragon had other ideas. The creature blasted through amid the protest of shredding fabric, wings forming faster than Zee thought possible. He pushed away from the too-small ledge, flapping furiously.

Chloe was already engaged in an aerial battle with two vampires. Fire spewed from her mouth, but it bounced off the pair. He trumpeted a battle cry and swung in close behind them. If they were warded, he'd have to get damned close. His dragon dive-bombed the vamps until they were close enough to touch. Time for fire to end these arrogant fuckers.

He belched dark smoke, hoping to cut off the vampires' air, make it tough for them to remain airborne and still maintain their spell. Chloe flanked him. *"I've got this,"* she screeched.

More fire flew from her. This time, her aim was true, or maybe she'd hit a chink in the vampires' defensive perimeter. Both the dark-robed horrors caught fire, turning into stinking, greasy pyres raining ash beneath them.

A quick glance showed the portal still disgorging vampires. What the hell? Had every vampire in the States showed up for this event? A blast of dark power rolled across the sky, followed by another.

Zachary wheeled, trying to sort out what was happening.

Chloe bugled, high, thin, frightened. He'd never heard a dragon sound that way. The portal bulged and pulsed as if something larger than the opening strained against it.

Eran and Yahn swooped near him. *"Fly with us. We must keep the Nachzehrer on the other side. It cannot enter our world."*

"What is that?" Chloe screamed the question.

"Soul sucker," Eran answered her. *"Part vampire,*

part ghoul. They used to be native to northern Germany."

Driven by outrage, fire roiled through Zee. He remembered the Nachzehrer all too well, but he'd thought them long since departed from Earth, along with a host of other monsters like the Laestrygonians, cannibal giants who'd hounded Ulysses.

The rot smell grew until every breath nauseated him. He flew after Eran, Yahn, and eight other dragons, with Chloe next to him. The Nachzehrer was partway out. Its upper body looked human—if any human weighed two thousand pounds—but its eyes were spinning black pools with brilliant crimson centers. Its lower body would be reptilian, but they couldn't let it push its way through.

The dragons fanned out, hitting the abomination with fire from different angles. Its hair caught fire, and it bellowed batting at the flame with hands tipped by long black talons. Poison oozed from them. Deadly nerve toxin that could kill in seconds.

"Do not get close enough for it to take a swipe at you," he screeched. The other dragons would remember, but Chloe didn't know.

She flew in a wide circle, keeping well out of range of the ghoul. Her vantage point offered her a perspective Zee lacked since his universe had narrowed to blasting the Nachzehrer with fire. Its hair was gone, and its skin had turned into a blistered, purulent ruin, but its eyes hadn't changed.

The abomination was already dead. Only silver, iron, fire, or beheading would do it in.

"It's a trap," Chloe screeched. *"Look above you."*

Zee flipped onto his back. Vampires were ranging themselves in rows above the dragons, but they were awkward in the air. Clumsy or not, their intent was clear. Drive the dragons close enough to the portal for the soul-sucking ghoul to reach them. All it had to do was break through a scale with those rapier-sharp, poisoned talons, and the dragon in question would die a grisly, excruciating death while flesh burned from its bones.

Ha! Two could play the vampires' game.

He banked, rolled, and beat his wings, gaining altitude, calling for Chloe to stay near him so they could fight together. The Nachzehrer was an equal-opportunity destroyer. It would mow through the vampires with as much gusto as it wiped out dragons. Intent on driving the undead lower, he took up a position above them.

Battle fever raged through him. He loved to fight. Dragons were born warriors. What the hell had he been thinking sequestering himself in a book-lined office?

His dragon bugled.

If Zee had been human, he'd have laughed. Flying was his destiny. So was fighting evil. Eran and Yahn joined him. The other eight dragons turned and flew as a group, rising higher after one last blast of coordinated fire at the ghoul.

Dark magic hit him from all sides but bounced off his thick, scaled hide. The vampires ranged below him might be arrogant, but they weren't stupid. He flew in formation with the other dragons, close enough their wingtips brushed each other. He made certain Chloe was between him and Eran. Between the two of them, they'd keep her safe.

The vampires twisted, trying to remain upright in the air so they could see the twelve dragons ranged above them, but their command of flight was so primitive, they couldn't maintain themselves other than belly down for long.

"Drive them down," Eran bellowed and dropped twenty feet. Fire blatted from him, and a vampire's robe caught fire. Absent his robe to maintain flotation, the horror couldn't fly, and he plummeted toward the ground.

Chloe mixed magic with fire, propelling the vampire right toward the ghoul.

"Grand idea," Zee bugled and mixed his power with hers.

Ancient, canny, and bloodthirsty, the nightmare

out of German mythology hooked out an arm that must have been twenty feet long and plucked the vampire from the skies, halting its precipitous dive toward Earth. With an unholy roar that shook the very foundations of the Victorian mansion, the Nachzehrer stuffed the vampire into its mouth, smoking robes and all. Its eyes spun with glee, and it bellowed something in German.

"*Gib mir mehr.*"

Ha. I'll give you more all right.

Zee followed the flight as they chivied the flying vampires downward. Rows of other vamps had squared off against mages and shifters on the ground. The vamps beneath them somersaulted from the air, joining their companions, and badly skewing the odds. Apparently, they weren't keen on turning into dinner for the Nachzehrer. Where the mages and shifters on the ground had been holding their own, now they were seriously outnumbered.

"*They need help.*" Chloe angled a wingtip toward the ground.

"*We have to shut that portal,*" Eran thundered. "*Once it's shut, we'll see what we have on the ground.*"

Smoke and fire belched from Zee. Eran would give him hell for this, but he told Chloe, "*Stand with your brother. I'll be there as quick as I can.*" He steeled himself, waiting for a stern rebuke from the flight leader, but it never came.

Eran was intent on one thing and one thing only. The portal. One dragon more or one dragon less wouldn't impact their strategy. Consuming the vampire had strengthened the Nachzehrer. It crawled another two feet out of the gateway, hissing and spitting.

"We can't kill it," Eran said. *"Not easily. Join your power with mine. We'll destroy the portal. It should take the Nachzehrer with it."*

Zee opened his magical center to the flight leader. Once they were linked, he felt the edges of the portal, the wrongness where it had invaded Earth. The gateway didn't belong here, so when Eran gave it a good, hard kick with their combined power, weaving earth magic in with his casting, it turned into a blazing inferno, shooting sparks hundreds of feet into the air.

"Keep it flowing," Eran urged. *"We're almost there."*

Sure enough the portal folded in on itself with a crashing, booming racket that made Zee's ears ring unpleasantly. Where there'd been a gateway, only a smoking hole remained. All traces of the Nachzehrer were gone. Belching smoke, his dragon didn't wait for Eran to release them. It slammed the door on their magic, banked, wheeled, and landed smoothly right next to Chloe. Still in dragon form, she added fire to the clank of iron blades as mages and shifters fought to get close enough to swing their weapons, beheading vampires as they went.

Still rank with evil, the air improved a little once the portal was gone, moving from full on charnel pit reek to decaying corpses. Zee tried to count, but he couldn't tell how many vampires remained. Stephan and Niall covered each other, closing for mortal blows with a couple of stragglers on the ends of the front line. Two swings. Two heads rolled in the dust. Black ichor spewed, coating everything. Grass. Dirt. Rocks.

Jeremiah prowled in cave lion form. If any vamps got close, he jumped on them, drove them to the dirt, and chomped through their necks. His tawny coat was mottled black with vampire blood, and his lion roared a battle cry.

Discordant notes sounded from the rear of the vampire ranks, sharp metal scraping over glass. The unpleasant squall rose in volume until Zee plugged his ears with magic.

Eran landed next to him. *"Goddess damn their eyes. They're leaving."*

"We have to stop them." Yahn touched down on Zee's other side.

A vicious maelstrom formed in the center of the vampire ranks. Black and whirling so fast everything close by got swept into its maw. *"Stand back."* Zee plopped his bulk right in front of Chloe.

"You too," she screamed.

The vortex clawed at him, dragged at him, but he had enough heft as a dragon to fight it.

"No!" Chloe shrieked and surged around him, intent on grabbing Sarai. The wolf shifter was being sucked toward the pulsing, throbbing evil.

Niall leapt after her, but Jeremiah planted himself in front of the jaguar shifter. *"Not going to lose you both."*

Niall feinted left, and then right. Jeremiah finally pinned him to a tree with one huge paw.

Chloe had scooped Sarai into her forearms and was fighting the maelstrom's pull. She was holding her ground, but not moving back toward safety. Desperate for his mate, Zee rose into the air and blasted the vortex with magic and fire. Eran had blotted out the Nachzehrer's portal with magic. Surely it would work on this joke of a fabrication. Eran, Yahn, and two other dragons joined him. All directed magic at the whirling horror that had Chloe and Sarai in its gunsights.

"Feed power right into the center," Zee shouted. The thing was weakening. He felt it falter, stumble, and collapse in a tower of stinking, noxious darkness.

Breath whistled through his clenched double rows

of teeth, and he plummeted to where Chloe stood, Sarai still in her arms.

Destruction spread out from the house, but the vampires were gone. Daylight was approaching. Of course, the craven bastards would leave.

Chloe set her friend down, and Niall ran to her, folding her into his arms.

"We won. For now." Chloe angled her whirling silver eyes Zee's way.

"Aye, that we did, although I fear the for now *part will be brief."*

"Doesn't matter." She dropped a wing across his back. *"I'll take my victories as I get them."*

"Fly with her." His dragon's command was crystal clear.

Chloe's jaws opened in the dragon version of a smile. *"That was an invitation if I've ever heard one. I accept."*

Steam rolled from his mouth, and he leapt skyward. If she was ready, so was he. He sent a blast of power to ease her way into the air, and she grabbed hold of it. Wings beating fast, she flew by his side. Unable to contain his eagerness for what was about to unfold, his cock shot to life.

The dragons' mating call bugled from him, and Chloe bugled back. Filled with need. Brimming with love. Hot. Ready. Soon she'd be his forever.

CHAPTER 12

A Few Minutes Before

Panic vied with terror and fury as Chloe watched Sarai get swept off her feet. She tried to shift to her wolf's body—the air around her incandescent with her efforts—but she couldn't pull magic fast enough. It would have meant letting go of where she'd dug her boots and hands into solid objects that ripped from the ground one by one.

After being frozen in place, Chloe bolted from behind Zachary, still awkward on her thick dragon hindlegs. Using her wings to help balance herself, she lunged for Sarai and bent low to grab her.

"Let go!"

"Save yourself," Sarai screeched. "I'll manage."

"Don't be an ass. I've got you."

Maybe because the bushes Sarai clung to uprooted

precipitously, she gave in. Chloe snatched her out of the dirt and cradled her against her scaled chest. Niall was screaming epithets from somewhere to her right, but Chloe had to concentrate. The vortex had upped its ante, and the drag against her was so strong it was scary.

This wouldn't be easy. She planted her rear talons into the earth, driving them deep. Fire shot from her mouth straight for the vortex, but the whirling horror sucked it in and burned brighter.

"Not a good idea," Sarai panted and shifted position to free one of Chloe's forearms.

"What am I going to do? Throw rocks at it?" Chloe quipped.

"Whatever works," Sarai countered.

Power flowed into Chloe; Sarai offering access to her magic.

The air felt wrong where it brushed against her scales. Her dragon bugled, trumpeted, and bugled again. It didn't send any more fire, though. Chloe focused all her magic, plus Sarai's, into a gargantuan effort and tried to back away from the whirling tower. She had to release her grip on the earth, though, before she could do anything.

Not the time for stealth or caution.

She wrenched one hindfoot free, intent on moving it back some. The suction from the maelstrom almost unbalanced her. If she sprawled on her ass, she'd be dead meat. Flying was out of the question. It took time to gain a toehold in the air. She'd be painfully vulnerable during those moments, and the hungry maw, glowing hotly, would nab her and Sarai.

She thrust her foot back to its original position, curling each talon around a clod of rocky dirt.

"No go, eh?" Sarai tried for brave but sounded rattled.

"Nope. We're here for the duration. Unless something changes and we catch a break." Chloe didn't go into how thin their margin was, how even a slight breeze might topple the cards against them.

Bugling dragons announced part of the flight was airborne. Zee, Eran, and Yahn positioned themselves dead center over the thing that wanted to eat her alive. Two more dragons joined them. Goddess only knew where she'd end up if she got sucked into the vortex. Not this world, and probably not any borderworld she could escape from.

Chloe fought harder. She did not want to die—or turn into one of evil's many minions. Plus, Sarai's fate hinged on her own. She had to hang on. For herself. For Jeremiah. For Sarai. For Niall.

For Zachary.

I love him.

The revelation shocked and thrilled her. Now that

her barriers were down, and she was fighting for her life, everything important sprinted to the front of the line. Mating with him took top priority—right after she extricated herself and Sarai from this mess.

"I'm sorry," Sarai said.

"Nonsense. Shut up. What was I supposed to do? Stand by while that black portal ate you?"

Above her, Zee and the dragons had switched up strategies and were shooting fire directly into the thing. Unlike her fire that had hit it broadside, theirs was changing the character of the chaos gateway. At first, she feared it might be expanding, but the thing shuddered.

Its pull lessened, not by much, but Chloe moved fast and slithered back two feet. *"Things are looking up."*

"I see that." A vicious undercurrent lined Sarai's words.

With no warning, no fanfare, the suction halted abruptly, and the glistening vortex fell in on itself. Breath puffed through Chloe's double rows of teeth in little panting gasps. Zee executed a tight turn and landed so close his wingtip brushed her shoulder.

Sarai wriggled against her. "Put me down, sweetie. All is well."

She'd no sooner settled Sarai on her feet than Niall

tore toward her, scooping her into a frantic embrace and ranting in Gaelic.

Chloe angled her gaze Zee's way. *"We won. For now,"*

"Aye, that we did, although I fear the for now *part will be brief."*

"Doesn't matter." She dropped a wing across his back. *"I'll take my victories as I get them."*

"Fly with her." Zee's dragon's voice blasted her.

She grinned. *"That was an invitation if I've ever heard one. I accept."*

Steam rolled from his mouth, and Zee leapt skyward. Extending her wings for balance, she ran a few steps flapping hard. Maybe someday she'd master the transition from earth to air without feeling like an awkward ninny. Power thickened the air beneath her wings. Power that smelled of the Scottish Highlands.

Zee was helping her, and she loved him for it. The woman she used to be would have resented the implication she couldn't manage on her own, but she had her priorities straight. Mating would seal her bond to Zachary. Maybe it would have helped him find her if she'd been swept into the maelstrom. Regardless, she rose smoothly into the air. He bugled a mating cry. A squeal twin to his issued from her throat.

Her dragon was all over this, and eagerness spilled through her.

Zee led her a few miles from home. Magic shimmered around them as he created a curtain, offering privacy. They spun, wove, dived, and spread their wings over and under one another's. He nipped her long, sinuous neck. She nipped back. When he flew above her and gripped her shoulders with his taloned forelegs, she was more than ready for the thrust that drove his cock into her. Colors flared all around them, and he held them steady midair and plumbed her, holding her just at the verge of cresting for delicious moments before he pushed her into a long, tumbling valley where passion held court.

Heat and desire and love mingled into a shining kaleidoscopic light show. *"I love you. The knowledge swept through me when I was fighting for my life—and Sarai's."*

A deep, lusty chuckle rolled through her mind. *"I love you too, lassie. Shall we finish this in bed?"*

She didn't know how to frame her question, so she blurted. *"Is this enough? Are we mated as dragons?"* If she'd been human, she'd have been tomato-colored.

He thrust deeper and laughed again. *"What do you think?"*

She snugged her unfamiliar dragon physiology around his erection. *"You're amazing. Incredible."*

"Keep it coming, wench. While you're at it, open your magic to me."

"Why? This is pretty damned magical all on its own."

"A surprise. You'll see."

Magic flashed and flared around them, brilliant with reds and oranges. She felt the shift magic altering them; at the same time the whole thing mixed into a travel spell. When the air stopped shimmering, they were naked atop her bed with his cock still deep inside her.

She'd thought herself strong magically, but the way he'd blended shifting and transporting them in one fell swoop blew her away. "Color me impressed, sir knight."

"At your service, fair maiden. Always." He flexed his cock inside her and made a distinctly male sound. Part possessive growl, part delighted yip.

"Mmmm." She pushed to her knees on all fours. Since he was behind her, it was a perfect position. Rather than thrusting, he withdrew and grasped her hips, turning her to face him as he knelt over her.

"I want to look at you." Heat from his blue eyes raked her from head to toe. Breath swooshed from his chiseled lips. "Damn but you are one gorgeous woman."

A quip about him saying that to all the girls died on her lips. Instead, she murmured, "Thank you." They were mates, stripped bare before one another's souls.

This wasn't a time to tease, and his compliment thrilled her. She wanted him to find her beautiful, just as she saw him.

He traced a line from the hollow between her collarbones to her breasts with his tongue, circling each nipple and sucking hard. Sensation, hot, sweet, bright, spilled through her.

She was already so aroused, she was stunned how much higher the touch of his mouth took her. She grappled for his cock but couldn't quite reach it. His mouth moved lower, tongue scribing her ribs, and then her stomach. When he fastened his mouth over her nub, she slithered around so she could lick the length of his erection. He tasted of salt and smoke and the acidic bite of semen.

He was doing wicked things to her with his teeth and tongue. She swiped his shaft with her tongue, and then laved the head with a series of little, biting kisses. He groaned and drove into her mouth. Encouraged, she did more of the same, gripping him with her hand to stabilize her efforts.

He inserted a hand between her legs, moving them wider apart as he plumbed her with his fingers, working her between his hand and his mouth. Passion swelled until her entire body turned into a swamp of lust, light, and sensation. The air thickened with sex and magic, and she dropped the last of her barriers,

accepting him completely into her heart, body, and soul.

He must have sensed the change, because his magic pulsed brighter, developing definite randy edges until the glow resembled an Old World bordello.

Thought deserted her as her body clawed for release. When she thought she couldn't possibly last a second longer, he swirled his tongue around the tip of her clit, and she exploded. Shock waves from her climax rocked her, and they just kept on rolling as he traded swirling for sucking.

She worked him harder, tightening her grip on his cock and jacking him faster. She threaded her other hand between his legs and teased the opening to his anus with a fingertip. He groaned, feral, possessive, and his already immense cock swelled still more before it shuddered in her mouth. She lapped semen, not wanting to lose so much as a drop.

They lay panting and gasping for long moments.

He slithered up her body and kissed her long and deep. She returned the kiss, loving how she tasted on his lips. Zachary broke the kiss, offering a sexy grin. "That position you took? The one where you were on all fours?"

She nodded, matching his grin—and his desire— with her own. "Yeah. Why?"

"Now might be a good time for it." He furled one red brow, regarding her.

"Guess you weren't kidding about us never getting out of bed."

"I never joke about what's truly important." He drew away, offering her space. "On your knees, my mate, my heart."

"How could I refuse?" She rolled onto all fours and arched her back, ready when he slammed into her. Even though he was gentle compared with when they were dragons, this was rough and tumble sex.

Just the way she liked it.

He drove into her hard and fast, and she met him with every stroke. When he reached around, taking a breast in one hand and rubbing her clit with the other, she shrieked her delight and hoped to hell no one was close enough to the third floor to overhear them.

They might be newly mated, but discretion never went out of style.

He stopped moving long enough to rock back and forth, maintaining just enough friction to delight her while he rubbed her nub in small, tight circles. Another climax seeded itself from her last one, and she melted around him, totally ceding control to her mate.

He teased her, loved her, brought her close, and backed her off. The next time when she was panting and heaving and doing everything she could to get him to move faster, goddammit, he finally did. The cock she lusted after took her, plumbing her to her core. She couldn't see him behind her, but she felt his hunger catch fire and willed him to come right along with her.

Magic shimmered around them, his mingled with hers as he made love with her. Her climax, so elusive because he'd held her back from cresting, ripped through her. She was still riding the waves when he juddered inside her, setting off a whole new orgasm.

They ground and strained against each other until the spasms died to ripples. She sank to the bed on her belly, and he turned them onto their sides, still glued to her body with his cock inside.

Warm breath laved her, along with steam, no doubt a gift from his dragon. Steam puffed from her mouth too. Happy little bursts from her very contented bondmate.

"I love you, lassie." His voice buzzed near her ear. "I vow to care for you, protect you. Our children too, if the world ever settles enough for us to have any."

She wanted to look at him, so she untangled herself from his body and turned onto her other side. Cradling his face in a hand, she said, "I love you too. We'll figure this out. Even if we have to pick off every single vampire one by one, we're bound to reach a place there aren't any more."

A wistful smile painted his face. "I don't want to

talk about vampires or evil or darkness. Not today. 'Tis our mating day. Can we banish the darkness until tomorrow?"

"Of course." It was more than fine with her. She'd like to banish vampires to a distant spot where she never had to think about them ever again.

They drowsed in each other's arms, trading kisses and endearments. Time passed. She had no idea how much, but at least daylight still filtered through the windows.

A staunch knock on her door snapped her eyes open. A reflexive jot of magic yielded Jeremiah—and Renee. "Sister. Sorry to bother you, but we're gathered downstairs."

Before she could reply, magic flashed, and Eran took shape next to the bed. Not nearly as respectful of their privacy as Jeremiah and Renee, who remained in the hallway, he grabbed Zachary's shoulder. "Enough rutting for one day, my boy. We need you at our war council. Up and at 'em."

Zee tightened his hold on her and twisted to gaze at the flight commander. "Five minutes."

"I'll hold you to it."

Zee rolled his eyes. "I suppose I should be grateful you gave us a few hours to ourselves."

Eran's serious demeanor broke apart, and he actually smiled. "The others have been holding me back. I'd have dragged you out of here as soon as you returned. The dragon mating was the critical one. All the rest was icing. Sweet, but totally unnecessary."

"See you downstairs," Jeremiah called.

"Get going." Eran took a step back but made no move to leave.

Zachary wrapped Chloe in the sheet like she was precious and rolled off the bed until he stood facing Eran. "We will dress and join you. Please offer my new mate privacy."

"Killjoy. I may have lost out to you, but I was hoping for a peek."

"Hope all you want." Zee leveled his gaze on the other dragon shifter. "Not going to happen."

Magic turned the air liquid, and the spot Eran had stood was empty.

Zachary darted into the bathroom and returned with a towel wrapped around his slender hips. "I'll be heading next door. Johnny's clothes are a fair enough fit, and I left mine in a pile of tattered fabric on the roof."

Chloe pushed back the covers and stood. "I'd love to shower, but I don't suppose there's time."

"No. Eran wasn't joking when he said the others held him back." Zee walked to Chloe and kissed her forehead. "No honeymoon for us. Not until we get the vampire problem under better control."

"It's all right. I have the most important thing."

"And what might that be, lassie?" He switched to Gaelic.

She mock slugged him. "Why you, of course. You already know that."

"Aye, but I never tire of hearing it."

Chloe understood because she felt the same way. Before she fell back into his arms, she hurried to her closet and dragged a set of sweats from one of the shelves. "See you downstairs."

"I'll only be one room over," he said. "Once you're dressed, stop by, and we'll go down together. Like a proper mated couple."

"I like it. I was missing you already."

"Of course ye were. We're joined, darling, soul to soul. Ye're heart of my heart, bone of my bone. We shall never be separate again."

"Is that part of the mating ceremony?" She shrugged into her hoodie and zipped it to her chin.

"Aye, 'tis indeed. We shall get to that part. Eran can marry us. He joins all dragon shifter couples."

"Five minutes," blasted into her mind.

"He's not very patient," she muttered.

"Nay, he's not. Patience isn't a dragon trait, nor is it valued among our people."

She balanced on one leg to draw on her pants. "You're patient."

"Only because I've lived long among humans." He shook his head, looking chagrined. "I'm going next door to find clothes. Left to my own devices, I'd never leave your side."

She blew him a kiss as he trotted out the door.

Joy welled, so thick she could almost taste it. Somehow, it felt wrong to be happy in the face of the vampire threat...

"It's not," her bondmate chimed in. *"Dragons are always at war. We take our joy as it finds us."*

It was good advice. She didn't try to argue her bondmate out of it. Chloe ran a brush through her tangled hair, stuffed her feet into ancient slippers, and ran lightly next door.

Zee's face lit with pleasure when he saw her. She grinned back from the doorway. "Come on. If I go to you and hug you like I want to, we'll never make it out of here."

"You're a wise woman, Chloe." He crossed the room in two long steps and hooked a hand beneath her arm. Together, they walked downstairs. No matter what happened from here on in, they had each other. It was the only thing that truly mattered.

You've reached the end of *Unbalanced*, book three of the Wylde Magick series. There's a lot of material to draw from in this world where vampires are on the offensive, draining magic—and blood—where they find it. Look for new Wylde Magick books through the end of 2018 and into 2019. Book four is already on the drawing board with a January release date. All I know so far is the hero will be a Capricorn.

Please, please leave a review for *Unbalanced*. Do it now while you're thinking about it. It doesn't have to be fancy. A couple of sentences would be great. Thanks so very much.

If you enjoyed this book, you might like my Soul Dance series. Full-length alternate-history, urban fantasy featuring shifters, gypsies, and vampires. An excerpt from *Tarnished Legacy*, one of the Soul Dance books, follows.

ABOUT THE AUTHOR

Ann Gimpel is a USA Today bestselling author. A lifelong aficionado of the unusual, she began writing speculative fiction a few years ago. Since then her short fiction has appeared in several webzines and anthologies. Her longer books run the gamut from urban fantasy to paranormal romance. Once upon a time, she nurtured clients. Now she nurtures dark, gritty fantasy stories that push hard against reality. When she's not writing, she's in the backcountry getting down and dirty with her camera. She's published over sixty books to date, with several more planned for 2018 and beyond. A husband, grown children, grandchildren, and wolf hybrids round out her family.

Keep up with her at www.anngimpel.com or http://anngimpel.blogspot.com

If you enjoyed what you read, get in line for special offers and pre-release special reads. Newsletter Signup!

Germany, 1940

Half Romani, Tairin's no stranger to hiding her mixed blood from gypsy caravans. What she can't hide is her perpetual youth, courtesy of her shifter heritage. Every few years, she drops out of sight, resurfacing in a new country to join a caravan where no one knows her. She's overstayed her welcome where she is, but Germany is at war, and travel has become all but impossible for everyone targeted by the Reich.

Elliott's clairvoyance is strong, even for a Romani. Seer for all the caravans in Germany, he catches Tairin eavesdropping outside their leader's wagon one night. He should turn her in, but it would mean her execution, and he can't bring himself to do that. Instead, he interrogates her. Her magic is different, but he can't figure out quite what she is.

Any association between Romani and shifters is forbidden, and Tairin shields herself from Elliott's probing. She should leave right now, tonight. It would be easy enough. Shift to her wolf form and run, keeping out of hunters' gunsights. She's on the edge of flight when Elliott suggests a covert task to prove her loyalty. Tairin agrees immediately, kicking herself for being weak where he's concerned. Shifters and Romani have no future together. Zero. Zilch.

She should be smart about this and vanish into the night—before he discovers what she is and destroys her.

January 1940

Munich, Germany

Elliott Brend moved his hands in a circular pattern over three lit candles, the stench of wax made from sheep fat sharp in his nostrils. Patterns danced like mad creatures on the walls of his grotto, and he chanted faster to bring his casting to life.

Darkness swirled, surrounding him. The candles guttered and died, their wicks drowning in pools of grease. Elliott bolted to his feet, hands extended, still working the spell he'd summoned. Fear thickened his tongue, but he couldn't stop now. Partially cast spells would make it possible for the demon he'd apparently conjured to drag him back to Hell with it. Usually this casting brought visions, not an actual entity.

The temperature in the grotto plummeted until ice crystals formed in the air. Wind wailed, thin and menacing. Shudders racked him.

"Why have you freed me? Not that I'm complaining, mind you." The words echoed around Elliott, chilling him further. "Speak, human. While you still can."

Elliott tried. Instead of words, a breathy croak emerged. He swallowed around his dry-as-dust throat. "F-future," he stammered. "What will happen? Many of the Rom have been captured."

Unholy laughter drove into Elliott's brain like overheated nails. It took all his self-control not to clap his hands over his ears, but if he did that, he'd be lost. His spell would falter, as would his tenuous hold on the demon. He'd be damned if he'd cede the upper hand to it.

Who am I kidding? It already has all the power it needs.

"You scarcely require me for future-telling," the disembodied voice said. At least the profane laughter had stopped. After the briefest pause, it added, "Flee while you can. Or the Rom will die out—here and elsewhere."

"Why do you care?" The words tore out of Elliott before he could stop himself.

"About your people? I don't, but magical energy will keep me on this side of Hell. Along with death. Fear helps too." A low, menacing chuckle punctuated the demon's words. "It's a perfect mix. You can blame the Nazis for my freedom. They provided an ideal medium. Coupled with your drawing spell, it allowed me to pierce the veil."

Elliott gathered power, letting it surge through him. The demon may have ridden in on the coattails of his earlier spell, but he couldn't allow it to remain. Too much evil was running unchecked as it was. Sparks crackled from his fingertips, burning him until his flesh smoked. The incantation, a surefire way to banish Hell's minions, crashed to the rotting wooden floor in a shower of glowing embers.

"Don't waste your magic, human."

"It's not a waste to return you to your proper place," Elliott snarled, wishing he could see the fucking thing.

"Try that last trick again, and you're a dead man."

Elliott sucked in a frustrated breath. He'd suspected the Rom were in serious danger. Signs they'd soon be targeted *en masse*, right along with the Jews, were impossible to ignore. All he'd sought this night was corroboration—and now he had it. He changed the cadence and timbre of his chant, hoping for an end to his spell, the hideous cold, and the abomination that scared the shit out of him. All he wanted now was for it to leave since returning it to Hell was beyond his ability.

"I am not leaving yet," the voice informed him. "You have no power over me, but you've already figured that out. Evil has risen. Rampant. Ubiquitous. As I noted earlier, it feeds me, right along with your magic."

Elliott clamped his jaws together to stop his teeth from chattering. What had he loosed on the world? "You must return at some point." He infused compulsion into his words. "If not today, or tomorrow, then surely soon. The dynamic balance between worlds will fail if you remain on Earth."

Laughter again. This time, it was even more loathsome and obnoxious.

"You haven't been paying attention, *human*. That dynamic balance? It's on its way out." Still laughing, the thing's foul presence receded.

Elliott sank into a crouch, mostly because his legs shook too badly to hold him upright. He wrapped his arms around himself and rekindled the candles with a jot of magic, welcoming their pools of light. Because it was easier than reconstructing what had just happened—and the wickedness now free because of him—he shuffled through options.

The demon's advice—if demons even handed out such things—had been to flee. But where? Austria, Poland, and Czechoslovakia were out of the question. Austria was a German ally. Both Poland and Czechoslovakia had fallen to German occupation a few months earlier. France would soon be under German rule. While his seer skills weren't absolute, he'd seen that particular event clearly.

Even if they could find a favorable location, how would they move the entire Romani population out of Germany? They still favored wagons, so any kind of stealth exodus was out of the question.

He rose to his feet and shambled to a window, gazing out at a moonless night. The elders from all the Rom groups in Germany had assembled a few days earlier, and they were waiting for him to return. Though they dealt in magic, his particular affinity for the darker side of the spirit world unnerved many of his kin.

Should he confess what he'd done?

He'd loosed wickedness eager to sign on with the blood-soaked Nazi regime, but how much worse could things get? He knew what the work camps really were, and so did the other Rom. None of his people fit the Aryan model of perfection, and their nomadic lifestyle was an affront to neat rows of impeccable houses where blonde wives raised blonde children in perfect obedience to the Reich's precepts.

Not much leeway for the Roms' brightly colored wagons or their sturdy horses. Their children who didn't go to school, or the canvas tents where they revealed futures, healed the sick, and fixed whatever was broken.

Bile splashed the back of his throat; he swallowed it down, and it burned all the way to his knotted belly. He still didn't understand how the Reich had mired Germany in such a chokehold, but it didn't matter. What did was ensuring Rom magic survived. It may have provided fodder for the newly released demon, but it also ensured the natural world would continue.

The traveling folk were tied to the world's beginnings in ways that had faded out of time and memory. They'd been run out of countries before and always endured, retooling themselves and keeping their magic under wraps as the world grew more modern.

If leaving Germany were impossible, they'd have to find a way to conceal themselves. The more he thought about it, the more the idea appealed to him. They faced evil, the likes of which the world had never seen. Evil that believed it could kill whomever it wished under the guise of cleansing the gene pool and producing a master race.

It would take gargantuan effort, but he and his kin could leverage magic to sabotage the Reich. Maybe even free the poor sods in those abominable camps. And make damn good and sure Germany went down in flames it would never recover from. Elliott had no idea if the elders would agree, but he'd float his idea. See if their philosophy, *Opré Roma*—Roma arise—was more than empty words.

Even if they don't agree, there's nothing that says I can't gather a few handpicked companions...

He curved his hands into fists until his nails cut into his palms. The more he rolled it around in his mind, the better he liked the idea of small vigilante groups that struck fast and hard, while remaining invisible to the *SchutzStaffel*, Germany's elite corps of political soldiers.

Determination straightened his spine. He dug a warm cloak out of the clothing chest leaning against one wall and wrapped it around himself before striding out of his well-hidden grotto located beneath the city. Part of a deteriorating tunnel system under a crumbling castle, his hideaway dated back to Roman times. He'd titrate what he told the elders until he saw which way the wind blew. Once he had a sense of that, he could make better plans.

Since none of them had stronger power than he did

to banish the demon, probably no reason to mention it at all...

He shook his head. Secrecy was a bad idea. He had to live with himself, which meant full disclosure. No matter how much shit he got for his folly.

Jairin Jabari prowled from one end of a clearing to the other in a forested glen. Her Rom family group had established a temporary camp here after local authorities ousted them from their previous location inside Munich's city limits. More than a dozen wagons fanned out in a circle, and horses were hobbled off to one side where grass grew thickly. Cars might be faster, but the smoky, noisy contraptions that always required repair had never appealed to Romani sensibilities.

She rolled her shoulders back to quell the creature sharing her skin. Her wolf wanted out, but it was too dangerous. For all their magic, power they scattered about like so much faerie dust, the Romani were superstitious about shapeshifters.

Worse than superstitious. They hated them.

She pulled her thick, black wool cloak tighter around herself and buried her hands in its thick folds. Her leather boots were soaked through, but it was winter. Short days and wet ground meant they never dried completely. Reaching within, she soothed her wolf, agreed its lush double coat and furred paws were far better suited to damp and cold than their current arrangement.

"*Promise me,*" the wolf spoke into her mind.

"*Anything, heart of mine.*"

"*Find us an hour when I can run.*"

Tairin closed her teeth over her lower lip, not wanting false words to fall between her and her bondmate. "*I'll do my best.*" Whether *her best* would yield the privacy required remained to be seen.

Something mollified the wolf. Maybe her words. Maybe her honesty. It withdrew to the place where it lived when it wasn't front and center in her mind.

She'd managed to hide what she was from the group she traveled with for the better part of twenty years. Soon it would be time to fade away—to find another country and maybe more Romani traveling companions. As it was, several of the women had made snippy comments about her perpetual youth. Tairin led them to believe she employed a glamour, but no one had the kind of magic to keep something like that going all day, every day, for years.

The sounds of male laughter, boasts, and glasses slapping a tabletop rose from the leader's wagon. He played host to eleven other elders this week. They'd gathered to discuss the evil that had descended on Germany. Elliott, the group's seer, was off doing goddess only knew what. Maybe he'd actually have a vision that would galvanize the Rom into something beyond business as usual.

Not a moment too soon, her inner voice muttered sourly.

If the disaster she suspected were imminent fell out the sky and onto their heads, they'd be rounded up. Herded into the death camps sprouting like cancers across what used to be the Prussian empire.

And that would be that.

She'd find a way through. Her wolf form would see to it. She could join one of many packs that howled their way through Germany's thick forests. But she'd become fond of the Romani after a rocky start. That and shared blood was why she'd traveled with several of their family groups for the past hundred years.

She wove her way into a thick evergreen grove where she wouldn't have to hide the anger that still filled her whenever she remembered how her people had kicked her out. Looking back was a dead end, yet once she'd begun, it took time to redirect her energy.

She was different from other shifters. And other

Romani. Born of a forbidden coupling between a wolf shifter father and a Romani mother, she hadn't been welcome in either camp once her powers blossomed. Her moon blood presaged her first shift, and her life had turned to warmed over crap right afterward. Shifters might have had more tolerance for how strong her magic was if her blood were pure, but it wasn't.

That she could shift at all meant the Rom wanted nothing to do with her.

Tairin took to her wolf form after being rejected by both sides of her kinfolk. She'd lived with local packs in northern Egypt for her first hundred years, give or take a few. Some alphas accepted her; others drove her away. She'd been between packs when a caravan of Romani wagons passing through attracted her attention, alerted her it was time to be human again. As a wolf, she was used to following her instincts without overthinking things. After so long, her animal nature was firmly entrenched.

So firmly entrenched, her first shift back to her human body took days to finesse. A Romani fortuneteller with Runic markings on her face and hands had found Tairin with her arms wrapped around her naked body, crying. After so long as a wolf, speech didn't come easily, so she'd had a ready excuse not to reveal that her tears were relief she still had a human form. Over the days she'd languished part wolf, part human, she'd been petrified she'd never find the purity of either body again.

The woman who rescued her moved her into the back of her wagon. As Tairin regained her very rusty ability to speak, she discovered the Romani group was on the move, traveling through Pakistan, Persia, and Turkey on their way to Romania. The journey had been hard and taken years. She'd stuck with them throughout, helping as she grew stronger. Though her new family wanted to know all about her, the only part she'd revealed was that she had some Romani blood.

She'd never repeated her past mistake about spending years in a single form. Her wolf had warned her it would be folly, but she hadn't listened to it. Nor did she assume her adoptive tribe would be tolerant if they knew what she truly was, so she dove headfirst into relearning Romani magic, remembering her affinity for it.

She'd been such an apt pupil she'd hidden just how potent her power was because she didn't want anyone to guess she was anything other than Romani mixed with human. As she'd developed her skills, she waited for the unknown to rise up and swallow her whole. Surely there was a reason the Rom avoided shifters. A reason why sexual congress was forbidden. Would her use of Romani magic leave her open to some hideous consequences?

Though she'd asked that question and others, taking care to be subtle about it, no answers were forthcoming. The lore books were written in Coptic, an old Egyptian language no one in her caravan seemed to have mastered at anything beyond a cursory level. Tairin spoke Coptic, but she'd never learned to read very well as a child, so translation was beyond her. Over the last century, she'd rectified being mostly illiterate, but her grasp of German and French didn't help decipher the lore books.

She stifled a frustrated sigh. Her current group of companions was the fourth one she'd joined since leaving Egypt. Given the rise of the Reich, it might well be the last.

The sounds of a horse galloping hard drew her back to the circle of wagons. Was Elliott returning? Or was an elder late to the party? She'd thought all were present and accounted for, but she might've been wrong. Tairin sent a slender thread of seeking magic outward. Elliott's energy resonated, making her heart flutter oddly.

The tall, broad-shouldered Rom with his long black hair and deep blue eyes moved with the grace of a large jungle cat. Seer power ran strong in him, and he dabbled in the darker side of Rom magic. Enchantments from Black Magick came easily to her, but she hid that particular ability from her fellows.

Sometimes she'd caught Elliott's gaze on her, sharply speculative. But if he saw through to what she was, he'd never said as much.

Elliott reined his horse to an abrupt halt, its thick hooves churning up clods of mud and stones. "Tairin." His voice rang with command and a surfeit of magic as he dismounted. "See to my horse." He tossed the reins her way and loped toward the wagon where the men held court. His leggy gait drew her gaze. He was so sensual, her body vibrated with wanting to throw herself into his arms. She'd never lain with a man, only with wolves, but she could imagine what it would be like.

Maybe it's time.

Maybe not. I got away with learning Rom magic. I might not be so lucky making love with one.

How would her half-breed blood react to joining with a Romani? She couldn't ask the question without giving away far too much about who she was.

She plucked the reins out of the dirt and sent soothing energy directly into the horse's mind. The stallion had been ridden hard. He needed a cool down, so she vaulted onto his back and walked him at a sedate pace until he stopped tossing his head and his breathing slowed. Some horses sensed her dual nature and resented the hell out of it, but the stallion seemed oblivious.

She'd tethered him near his fellows where he could graze and removed his saddle and bridle before curiosity drew her to the wagon where men's voices droned. Someone had shielded the conversation unfolding within, but she cut through the barrier with ease. Hunkering a few feet away, she eavesdropped shamelessly, wanting to know what would happen next.

Women fared better with the traveling folk than they did elsewhere, but Romani society was still run by men. When she sent her power spiraling outward to listen in on the men, the other women were all in their wagons, probably pretending all was well. The men—beyond the elders—milled about, busy with myriad tasks that needed doing each night. Younger children remained with their mothers. Older boys and girls helped the men do chores. Normally, they'd have set up their tents and wagons in Munich, soliciting local business, but the resident police force had made it abundantly clear they were no longer welcome.

Tension thickened the air. Even though everyone was acting as if tonight was just one more winter evening, they all knew better. Decisions unfolding one thin wall away from her would bind them to a course that might well spell their doom. A hissing snort bubbled up; Tairin smothered it fast before one of the elders heard and came out to investigate.

She swathed herself in invisibility and tilted her head, listening intently.

"You loosed a demon?" Michael thundered.

"How could you have been so irresponsible?" another voice she didn't recognize broke in.

"It's not as if that was my intent." Elliott's even baritone held a calming element. "I cast a scrying spell seeking visions, not one of Hell's minions." He paused for a few seconds, probably to strengthen the spell that lay beneath his words. "I did my damnedest to send the bastard packing. I wasn't strong enough, but we waste time speaking of him. We must decide how to proceed."

"Ye say the demon advised flight?" Stewart's Scottish brogue was unmistakable.

"Yes," Elliott replied.

"When we begin believing anything that emerges from a demon's mouth, we're finished," Michael said flatly.

"Och aye. Still, we canna remain here," Stewart said. "We canna work. We've been banned from the town."

"It won't be any different in Berlin or Heidelberg or Dresden," Elliott said. "The Reich have labeled our kind as undesirables. Our way of life is anathema to them."

"And ye know what happens next." Stewart's

words sounded like a dirge. "We join the others. The ones imprisoned by those Nazi bastards."

"Let me say my piece," Elliott cut in. "Then you can decide what's best for your individual groups."

"I'm not certain I want to listen to someone who let a demon loose to feed off the poison spreading across Europe," another elder grumbled.

"Your choice." Elliott spoke clearly, but without inflection. "My path is clear."

"Really?" Michael's single word dripped displeasure. "Last time I checked, you were part of my group, which means you're bound by my decisions."

Elliott cleared his throat. "Nowhere is it written that you own me, nor that I signed on with you for life. Look, men, we have a problem. If we continue to ignore it, the Nazis may well add us to their genocide list—"

"They already have," Stewart broke in. "I, for one, would like to hear what the lad has to say. Listening doesna bind us to action."

"Fine," Michael muttered dourly. "Proceed, but make it quick."

After a period of silence when Tairin held her breath, Elliott began to speak again. "Very well. Escape from Germany is unlikely given our numbers. A few of us might get lucky, but most of us will end up trapped. Neighboring countries aren't a haven. Either they're already occupied, or they soon will be." He inhaled noisily and blew it out. "Our only option as I see it is to hide. If we remain in our groups, they're manageable enough we might be able to pull it off."

"What aren't you saying?" Michael demanded. "I damn near raised you, Elliott. I know when there's more than what's come out of your mouth."

"I'm impressed." Elliott laughed softly. "You do know me, probably far too well. I plan to leverage my magic and do what I can to sabotage the Reich. I'm not certain how it will play out, but if I strike fast and hard, I can catch them off balance. By combining my seer ability and maybe astral projection or invisibility spells, I should be able to determine where my efforts will create the most damage."

"So will ye be doing this on your own, lad?" Stewart asked.

"If need be, yes," Elliott replied. "I admit, it would be better if a small group of us signed on, but this will be extremely dangerous, and I won't ask anyone else to risk discovery—and maybe death—if things go wrong."

"You might have discussed this with me first." Michael's tone held censure.

"When would I have had a chance?" Elliott shot back. "This idea only took shape today, after the demon left me to stew in my own guilt for having offered it free passage from Hell."

"Mmph. The way I see it," Michael said, "we have three choices. Business as usual. Attempt to make our way to somewhere the Nazi scourge hasn't touched. Or conceal our presence."

"That was my assessment," Elliott murmured.

"Ye did well, lad," Stewart said. "Now leave us so we may determine if we all bet on the same nag, or if we separate our fortunes."

Tairin had crept so close, she leaned against one of the wagon's wheels. The sound of scuffling footsteps as Elliott exited the wagon happened fast. Too fast for her to scamper into the forest. Barely breathing, she wound another layer of spells around herself, hoping invisibility would hide her presence. Once Elliott retired to the wagon he shared with three other unattached men, she could make her way to her own bedroll in one of the women's wagons.

Elliott trotted by where she crouched. He moved fast enough, she let herself hope she'd avoided discovery. Listening in on the elders, particularly after they'd shielded their conversation against prying ears, would surely earn her a session with the bullwhip. If not far worse.

For long, tense moments, she thought she'd pulled it off. She was just starting to breathe again when Elliott's heavy tread first slowed and then stopped.

Shit! Crap!

"Become me," her wolf piped up. *"We can knock him down and be gone before he knows what hit him."*

"We can't shift that fast."

Magic, shockingly strong, probed her perimeter. The gig was up. Elliott might not know it was her, but he realized something was next to Michael's wagon. Something that had no business there.

More power pushed against her invisibility spell, growing in intensity until he punched through. His magic ceased abruptly.

"Tairin!" ricocheted through her mind. *"I know it's you. Don't bother denying it. Get over here. Now."*

She rose to her feet, letting go of her spell as she moved to where he stood twenty yards away. She'd be damned if she'd cower, so she straightened her shoulders and stared him right in the eyes.

"Follow me," he ground out.

"Why should I?" she countered.

He spoke into her mind again. *"You have two choices. Either I call Michael, tell him what you were about, and let him decide what to do with you."*

"Or?" She feigned bravado she was far from feeling.

"We go someplace more private, and you tell me what the hell you were doing listening in on the elders' discussion." He narrowed his eyes to slits, but switched to speaking aloud. "I might still have to tell Michael.

Just so we're clear about that. I owe him allegiance. As do you."

Tairin jerked her chin toward thick timber. "Lead out."

Elliott shook his head. "Nope. You first. I'll be right behind you. And I warn you, if you try anything, I'll flatten you with magic and ask questions later."

She made her way to the grove of pines and firs where she'd been earlier. It was starting to drizzle, so she pulled her hood over her head. Tairin took her time as she worked on organizing which blend of truth might fly better. He'd be able to sniff out falsehoods right away.

His energy pounded against her back as she retraced her steps from earlier. She picked out anger, disbelief, and oddly enough, disappointment. Where was that coming from?

Tairin ducked beneath a low hanging limb and turned to face Elliott. It was dark, but her shifter blood meant she saw quite well in low light conditions. Elliott's dark brows were drawn into a thick, disapproving line.

"Talk and talk fast, sister."

The sizzle of power surrounded her, and she recognized a truth casting. "Was that really necessary?"

"What do you think?" His voice was low, tight

with something she couldn't interpret. "I find you swaddled in invisibility spells right outside Michael's wagon. You were obviously listening in. I want to know why."

"That's fair." She let go of her earlier intention of weaving a tale about idle curiosity mixed with boredom. Opening her eyes wide, she netted him with her gaze, trying her hardest not to pay attention to his high forehead, square jaw, and thick, curly hair that almost begged her to sink her hands into it.

"Come on, Tairin." He sounded exasperated. "Talk or you won't leave me any choices. What are you? A Nazi spy?"

Her mouth dropped open. "Awk. Jesus Christ! Oh, hell no." She bristled. "I have eyes and ears. I see what's going on about us. If you must have the truth, I was thinking about leaving, setting out on my own because I could hide myself better that way."

The edges of his magic probed her again. Along with it, his scent rose, tickling her nostrils with bay rum and piquant vanilla. She couldn't help herself, she breathed deep, inhaling the maleness of him.

His power jabbed her when he delved deeper. She rubbed her forehead. "Ouch. Surely that's more than enough. You must've picked up truth in my words."

"I did." Without warning, he closed the distance between them and clasped her head between his hands, pushing her hood back onto her shoulders. Rain pounded from the sky, soaking her.

The intense nearness of him made her knees weak, but she struggled, trying to get away. In all her years with the Rom, the only one who'd touched her had been that first fortuneteller, and the woman had a kind heart. She hadn't suspected a thing, and her touch was aimed at healing, not peeling back the layers of a secret Tairin had guarded for years.

"Stop!" She writhed in his grip.

His scent intensified, and the air around them turned silvery, glistening against the raindrops. Before he could dig deep enough to discover what she was, she wrapped her arms around his neck and pulled his mouth atop hers. The touch of his lips set fire to her blood, and she tightened her hold on him, kissing him as if the fate of the world rested on never letting go. Desire hot enough to set her heart racing sent sensation spilling through her.

After the briefest of hesitations, he buried his hands in her hair and sank his tongue inside her mouth. Something about the way he fell headlong into her embrace made her suspect he'd imagined kissing her just like this.

Whatever works. If this keeps him from unraveling my secrets, it's a small price to pay.

But she was deluding herself. She couldn't make

love with him without telling him what she was. He'd never forgive her. More importantly, she'd never forgive herself.

His cock swelled against her belly, rigid with need. What would he look like? Taste like? She ached to wrap a hand around that hardness and drag him inside her body.

Reluctantly, she tore her mouth from his and let go of him. "Sorry," she managed through panting breaths. "I don't know what got into me." She stole a quick glance upward through lowered lids before adding, "I— I'm a maiden. Not a harlot."

"I know." His voice throbbed with yearning. "But you're right that this isn't a good idea. Not with all the problems we face."

She wasn't sure whether to agree, so she held onto a wary silence. Where would this go next?

He let go of her head. "Your magic is strong. As strong as any Rom I've ever come across. Yet you're not full blood."

She licked her swollen lips, anxious to change the subject to something other than her power. "I could help you."

"With what?"

She rotated one hand in a circle. "That plan you described. My magic is potent, and it would complement yours since I'm female."

"Hold on." He shook his head. "I was trolling for men. Women don't go to war."

"The hell they don't." She shook wet hair out of her eyes. Annoyance scoured her nerves, and she stuck out her chin. "Try me. If I don't pass muster, I'll either join the women and sew doilies, or more likely, I'll slip away and wage my own mutiny against the Reich."

His chiseled lips, lips she was having a hell of a hard time resisting, twitched into a smile. "You're on, woman. Feel like a ride?"

"Where are we going?"

"Somewhere we can plan our first offensive."